SOLDIER

AIR RAID SEARCH AND RESCUE

DOGS

READASLL THE

SOLDIER DOGS

BOOKS!

SOLDIER
AIR RAID SEARCH AND RESCUE
DOGS

MARCUS SUTTER

ILLUSTRATIONS BY PAT KINSELLA

HARPER FESTIVAL
An Imprint of HarperCollinsPublishers

HarperFestival is an imprint of HarperCollins Publishers.

Soldier Dogs #1: Air Raid Search and Rescue
Copyright © 2018 by HarperCollins Publishers

Library of Congress Control Number: 2018934065
ISBN 978-0-06-286866-4 (trade bdg.) — ISBN 978-0-06-284403-3 (pbk.)
Typography by Celeste Knudsen
18 19 20 21 22 PC/LSCH 10 9 8 7 6 5 4 3 2 1
❖
First Edition

To Joel Ross
And to all the brave people and dogs
who did their part during WWII

CHAPTER 1

Twelve-year-old Matt Dawson hunched in the darkness as bombs fell outside the half-collapsed movie theater. He hugged his knees in the cramped space beneath a fallen balcony. His breath came loud and panicked. He was trapped.

He could hear his ten-year-old foster sister, Rachel, trying to stifle her crying nearby, but he couldn't see her. Rubble surrounded them both. There was no way out. Sweat pricked Matt's skin, and the air was clogged with smoke and dust.

He heard the shriek of air-raid sirens and the

groan of a wall collapsing. How long before the rubble fell on him and his sister?

He wanted to give up, but he needed to be brave for Rachel, just like his brother, Eric, used to be brave for him. He didn't feel brave, though. All he felt was scared. Still, he stretched his arm through the rubble until his fingertips barely touched Rachel's.

"It's going to be okay," he told her, but he didn't really believe it.

Matt was American. His parents had brought him to England so his father could help with the war effort. Then the entire family had moved to Canterbury to escape the air raids in London. But the raids had changed targets, and now he and Rachel were trapped inside a ruined movie theater and the bombs were still falling.

Nobody could find them. Nobody could save them.

"Do you think the raid is over?" Rachel whispered into the darkness.

"Maybe. Or maybe there are more waves coming."

"There can't be! When will it stop? When will— Oh!"

"What?"

"I think I heard people!" Rachel took a breath. "Help! Help!"

"We're in the movie theater!" Matt yelled, even though he didn't hear anyone. "We're trapped!"

He heard a shout from the street, muffled by the rubble. A bunch of voices that sounded like firemen, desperately battling a blaze. Firemen like his brother, Eric.

"Help!" Matt yelled. "We're trapped!"

"There's nobody in the movie theater," a man's voice said.

"Are you sure?" another voice asked.

"In here!" Matt called. "Hello?"

"We're trapped!" Rachel shouted, in her accented voice. "Help!"

The men couldn't hear them through the rubble. Not with the sirens screaming and the fires roaring.

"It's all clear," the first man said. "Move out."

"No!" Matt shouted. "WE'RE IN HERE!"

The voices faded away . . . then Matt heard a distant barking.

"Chief!" Matt shouted. "Chief!"

Chief's barking grew more urgent.

"Chief!" Rachel yelled.

"What is that mutt doing?" the first man said. "We've got a situation around the corner. Get a wiggle on!"

"Drag him along," the second man said, when the barks became sharper. "There's nobody in the theater. The mangy fleabag just wants to watch a movie . . ."

Matt and Rachel screamed and shouted, but the voices grew fainter and fainter.

Until they disappeared—even Chief's.

And Matt and Rachel were alone. Again.

CHAPTER 2

SEVEN HOURS EARLIER

"**C**lean the table," Matt's mother told him after dinner.

Matt paused in the door to the hallway. "It's Rachel's turn."

"Rachel's doing her homework," his mother said.

"I'm walking the dog!" Matt trotted toward the side door, yelling over his shoulder. "I'll do it when I get back!"

"Don't go too far," his mother called after him. She'd been on edge for a month, ever since the Germans threatened to bomb historical sites in England. They *lived* in a historical site: the ancient city of Canterbury.

Before Matt reached the door, Chief loped beside him from the other room. Matt wasn't surprised. Chief always showed up when you needed him. Matt's older brother, Eric, used to always be there too. But once the United States entered World War II, Eric had joined the Marines and shipped out. He'd left Matt to look after Chief: a strong, smart, loyal German shepherd–collie mix.

Matt grabbed the leash from the rack. "C'mon, boy!"

Running outside, he heard his mother saying something about the dishes. He felt bad for taking off, but he'd promised Eric that he'd take care of Chief. Also, he hated cleaning the table.

Especially when it was Rachel's turn.

Matt's mother had been a schoolteacher in Minneapolis before they'd come to England. After the schools closed in Canterbury, she'd started teaching Matt and Rachel herself. Which was okay, except Rachel got extra classes in English, which meant Matt got extra chores.

Also, Matt missed spending time alone.

Well, what he *really* missed was spending time with Eric. Back in the States, his brother had played football and studied engineering, just like their dad. He'd worked as a fireman in the US, and after they'd come to England, he'd volunteered as one.

But despite being busy, Eric always found time to toss a ball around with Matt, to teach him Morse code and take him to a movie or for an ice-cream cone.

Then he'd joined the Marines. He hadn't even waited to be drafted! He'd just gone to the US Embassy in London and enlisted.

He left the family—left Matt—months before anyone told him he had to. And the last thing he'd said to Matt was, "Take care of Chief."

"What about everyone else?" Matt had asked.

"If you take care of Chief," Eric had said with a wink, "*he'll* take care of everyone else."

Except, after shoving through the side door, Chief was more interested in peeing on a bush.

"C'mon, boy," Matt told him. "Before Mom finds us."

Matt and Chief trotted down the street and across the lawn of an ancient building that loomed high overhead. Matt loved the old stone structures around Canterbury—especially the still-standing sections of the city walls. With round towers and heavy stones, they reminded him of castle fortifications.

Which, according to his brother, they actually were. The Romans had built forts here in Canterbury almost two thousand years earlier. Matt liked to imagine Roman soldiers with shields and spears patrolling the wall and charging into battle.

Matt picked up a stick and threw it across the lawn. "Fetch!"

Chief charged away and returned holding the stick between his white teeth. He gave Matt a playful, teasing look, like he wasn't going to give him the stick.

"You've got to drop it if you want me to throw it again," Matt told him.

Chief shook the stick once, then dropped it at Matt's feet.

They played fetch until Chief lost interest and relieved himself again on a stone wall.

"Have some respect for history!" Matt told him.

Chief watched Matt with his dark, clever eyes. He was a big dog with a glossy coat, white teeth, and a pink tongue that lolled from his mouth when he panted. He sometimes scared people who didn't know him, but he also liked lying on his back and having his tummy rubbed.

And most mornings he'd steal Matt's pillow, drag it onto the floor, and curl up tight, trying to fit his whole body on it. He always hung over the edges, but he never stopped trying.

Matt reached down and scratched behind one of his pointy ears. "Another boring night. I wonder what Eric's doing right now."

Chief cocked his head, like he recognized the word "Eric."

"You miss him, boy? I miss him too."

Chief whined faintly.

"Don't worry," Matt said. "Eric's okay. He's probably off fighting the Japanese right now."

Chief nuzzled his hand and looked toward the house.

"Fine," Matt said. "I'll clean the table. But

don't pretend you're so helpful. I know you just want to lick the plates."

He started toward the house, and a shape drifted from the shadow of the wall. Chief gave a warning bark, and Matt's heart squeezed in fear. All of his parents' worries washed over him: about staying in England, about raising kids in Canterbury with the Nazis rampaging across Europe.

Chief lunged toward the shadowy figure, never hesitating to protect Matt—

And Rachel's giggles sounded through the night as Chief licked her face.

"Down, Chief!" she said, in her accented English. "You silly bear!"

"What're you doing here?" Matt demanded. "You're supposed be finishing your homework."

Rachel ducked her head, and her curly dark hair fell around her pale face.

"Would you stop following me around?" Matt said.

"Your mother is wanting you," Rachel said.

"I know! That's where I'm going. C'mon, Chief."

Chief gave Matt a look and stayed with

Rachel, brushing his muscular side against her skinny knees.

Rachel twined her fingers in his thick fur.

Matt grumbled. Chief was Eric's dog. Why did he spend so much time trying to cheer *Rachel* up? She needed her own dog. Or even a cat!

Anything so she'd stop tagging along with *him*.

Back inside the house, Matt cleared the table, then flopped onto the couch in the living room. His father wasn't home yet. That wasn't unusual. His father often worked late into the night, busy on some hush-hush engineering project with his colleagues in the British military.

When Matt's family first came to England, they'd lived in London, which was the biggest city Matt had ever seen. They'd left after the first wave of air raids, when the government started evacuating kids to the countryside—including to Canterbury.

So they'd moved here, into a little house between the cathedral and the city center.

Except six months after *that*, the government had evacuated the same kids out of Canterbury and shut down all the schools. They were mostly sent to the north of England. Matt's family had stayed that time. His dad couldn't move that far from work, and his mom refused to leave again.

"I'm not letting the Nazis chase me out of another house," she announced.

Matt guessed that she'd had another reason for wanting to stay. He figured she wanted to let Rachel stay in one place for a while, instead of always moving to new towns. Maybe that would help with Rachel's nightmares.

Rachel had come to England a few years earlier, through the Kindertransport program, which rescued Jewish kids from Nazi-occupied countries. The program helped thousands of children flee to England from Eastern Europe before the Germans killed them—but it was only for kids. The immigration laws kept their parents and grown-up brothers and sisters from joining them.

A few months ago, Matt's parents had brought Rachel to live with them. She was quiet and shy. Matt didn't mind her, really, except she was always *there*. Like a shadow. She never left him alone.

Mostly, though, he just missed Eric. And he

had a secret. One that he'd never told anyone except Chief.

He was mad at Eric for enlisting so early. He was mad at his parents, too, for letting him go. He never said anything, because he didn't want to seem selfish or unpatriotic, but every night he went to bed angry.

"I can't believe they let Eric enlist," he grumbled to Chief as he buttoned his pajamas that night.

Chief's ears pricked, and he sniffed toward Matt's pillow.

Matt flopped onto his bed. "He could've waited."

Chief snurfled at the sight of Matt's head on the beloved pillow. Abandoning his goal of stealing it, he turned in circles, then lay beside the bed.

Matt yawned and said, "See you in June," because it was the last day of May, and it would be June 1st in the morning.

He tossed and turned for a while before falling asleep. And he woke shortly after midnight, when the air-raid sirens shattered his dreams.

CHAPTER 3

12:05 A.M.

Matt burst into the hallway in his paja-mas, heart pounding. Chief was already in Rachel's room, barking to wake her.

"Shoes and coats!" Matt's mother called. "Front door!"

Matt knew exactly what she meant, because they'd prepared for an air raid. He galloped down the stairs. He flung open the closet and grabbed his coat, Rachel's, and his mom's. "Where's Dad?" he bellowed.

"He's still at the office!" his mom called back.

Dad worked with a bunch of military types, so they had a great air-raid shelter at his office—but his absence still made Matt a little nervous.

He shook his head. Eric wouldn't get nervous. Eric would spring into action.

He shoved into his shirt and slipped on his boots.

"Are they here?" Rachel ran down the stairs in her nightgown, her thick braid swinging halfway down her back. "We have to hide!"

"Nobody's here," Matt said, and helped her into her coat. "It's just an air-raid siren."

Rachel's face was pale. She looked so scared that Matt grabbed her hand. Not because he liked holding hands, of course! But Eric had once held his hand during an air-raid drill, and it had worked. He'd felt safe.

"Don't worry," he told Rachel. "The shelter's right nearby. There's plenty of time."

She took a shaky breath and squeezed his hand. Then Chief barked, and his mother, only halfway inside her coat, threw open the door. "Children, run to the cathedral! I'll be along in a flash."

"We're supposed to stick together!" Matt said.

"You said if there's an air raid we need to stick together."

"I know, sweetie—but Mrs. Lloyd might need help."

Mrs. Lloyd lived next door, and she was pregnant. She was *very* pregnant.

"You remember where to go?" his mom asked.

"Sure," Matt said. "The shelter under the cathedral."

"Take care of Rachel."

"I *know*," he said. "C'mon, Chief!"

When he led Rachel outside, the air was cool on his cheeks. The rising-and-falling cry of the sirens sounded louder.

Chief ran ahead, then looked over his shoulder and barked, urging Matt to follow.

"We're coming!" Matt said.

A door slammed down the street. It sounded like a gunshot, and Rachel jerked to a halt and gasped something in Polish or Yiddish.

"C'mon!" Matt snapped, but when he looked at Rachel, he saw terror in her eyes. "Oh! Um . . ."

The siren shrilled, and Rachel stared down the street, her hand trembling in Matt's.

Matt asked himself what Eric would do. He'd probably give Matt a job. That would keep Matt busy, so he'd forget about being scared.

"Uh, tell Chief we're coming, Rachel. He'll believe you."

After a moment, she nodded. "We're coming, Chief!"

Chief lowered his chest to the ground and wagged his tail, like he wanted them to chase him.

Matt and Rachel followed him into the darkness. There were no lights from the buildings. The entire town—the entire *country*—was dark at night, every single night, so the German bombers couldn't find targets. There were no streetlights. Everyone draped thick "blackout" curtains over their windows. Even the ambulances had hooded headlights, to keep them invisible from above.

The buildings were spooky in the pitch-black, but the darkness meant they were still safe. Matt had read that German planes dropped flares to light up their targets so the next waves of bombers could attack them, using incendiary firebombs that burst into superhot flames and five-hundred-pound high-explosive bombs that detonated in terrible blasts.

"Stay calm!" an air-raid warden called. "If you don't have a shelter, head for the cathedral basement." Two dark figures rushed past nearby, while down the block people called to each other, rushing into the cool summer night and heading for shelter. The siren continued to wail.

Matt squeezed Rachel's hand and followed Chief to the end of the street—and that's when he heard them.

Engines.

Airplanes.

A wave of German bombers.

Matt's stomach ached, and his teeth chattered. He tightened his grip on Rachel's hand and followed Chief faster down the street. When a soft whistle sounded from the darkness, Chief gave a warning bark, raced ahead, then dashed back.

There were already bombs in the air! They were tumbling through the sky, coming closer every second.

What if they hit nearby?

What if they exploded on top of Matt and Rachel?

With a whuffle, Chief veered into a shortcut along a path behind a brick building. The whistling grew louder as Matt followed onto the next street, ran around the corner—

And froze.

The Canterbury Cathedral loomed atop the hill in front of him, glowing with a brilliant yellow-and-orange light. Stone towers rose into the sky, and weird shadows danced across the ornate walls. It was grand—like a fairy-tale cathedral.

Except at nighttime, in the middle of a war, Matt shouldn't have been able to see any details. The colorful glow was beautiful . . . and dangerous.

The shelter was underneath the cathedral, and the Germans were trying to destroy it!

CHAPTER 4

Chief felt the girl's little fingers curling into the fur on his neck. He wouldn't allow just anyone to grab his throat like that, but Rachel was only a pup.

Plus, she was scared.

Even more scared than usual. Chief could smell it.

Chief always took care of his pack. If that meant fighting or hunting, he'd fight or hunt. If it meant nuzzling a scared pup, he'd do that too.

The girl-pup startled at sudden sounds. She whimpered in her sleep. She was quiet and scared, but she was strong too. Chief smelled that in her.

The boy-pup was strong in a different way. Chief twitched his coat thoughtfully. Matt was not quiet, though: he reminded Chief of himself as a pup.

The mother and father were just old. Chief always tried to let them pretend they were in charge, but other than that, they could take care of themselves.

Chief missed the other member of his pack. The older boy had raised Chief. Eric. He was partly a father to Chief, partly a brother, and partly a pup.

The humans couldn't hear the loudest noises, they couldn't smell the strongest scents. They shivered in the wind and barely had any teeth at all.

They were so useless sometimes!

They needed a dog to look after them. That was okay, though. A pack always looked after each other. That's what made a pack a pack.

The rumbling of the iron birds in the night sky sounded louder, and the whistling of the fire-rocks made Chief growl deep in his throat. He prowled behind the boy-pup and girl-pup, urging them to go faster—but the girl-pup stopped at the sight of the flame-lit building.

She yipped in fear. The boy-pup smelled almost as scared, but he took a deep breath and said, "We need to head inside, Rachel. Like Mom said."

"We stick together?" the girl-pup asked.

"I couldn't get rid of you if I tried!" Matt said, and smiled at her.

She didn't smile back.

She stood frozen in place until Chief nudged her. Then she let Matt take her toward the line of older humans just . . . standing outside the big building. Waiting to get into the underground den that Chief smelled. But they were hardly moving!

He barked at Matt, telling him to push past the old people and get inside.

"Quiet, Chief," Matt said. "We're in the queue. You can't rush the English; they love waiting in line. We'll get there."

Two older females turned and beckoned to the kids. Rachel nervously stroked Chief's back as they joined the crowd. He smelled fear coming off her in waves and pressed closer.

Matt must've smelled her fear, too, because he spoke in a soothing purr. "I remember the first time Eric took me to the cathedral. I thought it'd be a musty old church. I asked if we couldn't just throw stones into the river instead."

"S-silly boy," Rachel said. "Throwing rocks at water."

Matt herded Rachel through the crowd toward the entrance. "Eric said the cathedral would really knock my socks off. And it did. My socks were completely knocked. I mean, all the stained glass and nooks and crannies and statues." He gestured toward the big stone building. "But do you know what's inside there now?"

Rachel shook her head. "The air-raid shelter?"

"Well, that's underground. But inside the normal sanctuary, I mean? The floor is covered in dirt. Huge mounds of dirt, like the biggest sandbox in the world. Heaped inside this ancient cathedral. I laughed when Mom showed me."

"Why all the dirt?" Rachel asked, her fear-smell fading.

Chief nudged Matt with his snout. He'd done well, soothing Rachel.

"That's what I asked!" Matt said, scratching behind Chief's ear. "Mom says it's to protect the air-raid shelter."

Rachel wrinkled her nose. "How does dirt protect the shelter?"

"Because the shelter is underground, beneath the cathedral floor. Which is now covered in truckloads of dirt, like ten thousand sandbags."

"So a bomb would have to blast through all that dirt before it reached the shelter?"

"Exactly!" Matt smiled. "And the shelter's really strong too. It's in an ancient crypt! Isn't that *aces*?"

"What is a crypt?"

Matt paused. "Oh, just like a really safe cellar. But the dirt on the floor overhead will protect it from bombs and stuff."

The roar of the iron birds rumbled from above. Too loud. Too close! Chief barked again and lunged forward, opening a path to lead Matt and Rachel through the crowd.

A shriller whistle sounded as a fire-rock plunged from the sky. Chief needed to get the kids inside. He needed to keep them safe!

CHAPTER 5

"**S**orry!" Matt told the people in the crowd as he followed a lunging Chief toward the crypt. "Sorry!"

The startled British faces around him looked angry at first—then they realized that Matt and Rachel were kids and hustled them toward the door.

"Shake a leg, Rachel!" Matt said.

She peered at him. "Shake my leg?"

"It means *hurry!*" he explained, pulling her forward.

The sound of the German airplanes faded when Matt and Rachel rushed inside the stone doorway. The adults pointed to a stairwell leading underground toward the crypt. Which wasn't actually just a deep cellar, like he'd told Rachel. It was more of an indoor cemetery. In the old days, they'd buried people there.

When Matt first heard about the crypt, he'd imagined cobwebs, skulls, and creepy old tombs. It wasn't like that at all. Instead, it was a huge rectangular room with rows of stubby stone columns. Lanterns cast a yellow glow on the dozens of people in the room. More arrived every minute, some carrying blankets and pillows and thermoses. One old man had even brought a sandwich.

At Matt's knee, Chief gazed at the sandwich and wagged his tail hopefully.

The old man didn't seem to mind, but Matt noticed other people giving Chief dirty looks. There hadn't been enough food for the *people* of Britain during the war years, much less for dogs. The government only allowed every family a couple of ounces of sugar and butter and cheese per week, and a few pounds of meat.

In fact, Matt had heard that dogs weren't really allowed in air-raid shelters. Nobody said anything to him, but he felt his cheeks warm. He wasn't about to leave Chief outside in the middle of a bombing.

"C'mon, Chief," Matt muttered.

He slunk toward a dark corner of the crypt where nobody would notice them. Rachel followed, of course.

"Where is your mother?" she asked, tugging nervously at her braid.

"She'll be here," Matt said, and leaned against a column to watch the entrance.

"It is not good to be away from the parents," Rachel said.

Matt almost made a dumb joke about not having to wash the dishes. But Rachel had left her parents behind when she'd come to England. Her parents and her older sisters. Her uncles and aunts and cousins—her home, her friends, her entire life.

She still had nightmares about saying good-bye. About leaving everyone she loved behind in

Nazi-controlled Europe. She'd probably give anything to hear her mother telling her to clean the table.

So Matt kept his mouth shut. And he felt suddenly nervous, like Rachel's fear was catching.

Where was his own mother? She said she'd be right behind them, but she was nowhere in sight. They were supposed to stay together if the sirens sounded—that was their plan—and they'd already lost each other!

Matt chewed on his lower lip and stared at the door.

He tried to stay brave. He was twelve years old, after all, not some little kid. He'd traveled all the way from Minnesota, USA, across the ocean to England.

Plus, Eric always said Matt was tough—and he wasn't going to let Eric down.

Still, he kept searching the room, hoping that his mom was already in the crypt and that he'd missed her. Strange scrapes echoed, voices murmured, and lantern light flickered creepily.

When Chief nudged him with his furry head,

Matt felt a flash of hope. Maybe Chief had seen his mother! Matt rose onto his tiptoes and peered toward the door.

Someone was coming!

But when Matt caught a glimpse of the person through the crowd, he deflated. It wasn't his mother. Instead a bearded man in pajamas stepped into the shelter and shouted, "The bombers are getting closer!"

CHAPTER 6

A fearful hush fell across the shelter.

Matt's breath caught, and his fists clenched. What if a high-explosive bomb scored a direct hit on the cathedral? Would a bunch of extra dirt be enough to protect them?

But an instant later, the hush ended. Conversation returned. *Calm* returned, and an easy confidence spread through the room. One thing that Matt had noticed about the British, they weren't very good at panicking. *He* still felt a little panicky, though, trapped in a crypt during an air raid without his parents.

Chief nudged Matt again.

"What, boy?" Matt's worried gaze flicked downward. "You still can't have a sandwich."

Chief gave a short yip and looked intently at the door.

And to Matt's relief, his mother entered, helping Mrs. Lloyd into the shelter. Matt almost laughed in relief—and almost laughed again when he saw Mrs. Lloyd. She was wearing Matt's father's woolen hunting cap with ear flaps. His mom must've wanted to keep her head warm in the chilly June night.

"There she is!" he blurted, a little too happily. "Not that I was worried."

Rachel exhaled. "It is good she is here."

"Stay with Chief," he told Rachel, and trotted across the crypt.

He slipped between the columns to the small crowd around his mother. He squirmed through and found Mrs. Lloyd lying on one of the few bunks. Despite the cool crypt air, her face was glossy with sweat beneath his father's woolen hat.

A bunch of ladies stood around the bunk. One

of them was stringing up a clothesline to hang a curtain for privacy. Another chatted with a priest from the cathedral. Matt felt a spark of pride that his mother was the one holding Mrs. Lloyd's hand.

"Mom!" he said, squeezing forward.

"There you are, sweetie!" His mother shot him a distracted smile. "Find a place to settle in where you aren't in the way."

"Aren't you coming?" he asked. "We're supposed to stay together. That's the plan."

"I need to stay with Mrs. Lloyd right now."

Despite her pale face, Mrs. Lloyd smiled as she offered Matt the woolen hat. "I'm afraid I need to borrow your mother longer than I borrowed your father's hat."

"Um." Matt took the hat and looked past Mrs. Lloyd to his mother. "You told me a million times. 'If there's an air raid, stay together.' Now Dad's not even here, and you're—"

"Matt, please!" she said, a warning note in her voice. "Not now."

"Fine," he grumbled. It wasn't fair, but that

didn't surprise him. Nothing was fair when you were a kid.

"Thank you. Now you look after Rachel." Her gaze moved past Matt's shoulder. "And *you* look after Matt."

When he turned, he found Rachel at his elbow, chewing on the tip of her braid, with Chief standing beside her. Great. First his mother scolded him when *she* was the one ignoring the air-raid plan, then she didn't even say anything about Rachel wandering around.

One of the women gave Matt an armload of blankets and shooed him away.

He stalked toward the column in the corner. "I told you to stay there!" he told Rachel.

She didn't answer. She just tagged along like always.

"At least we have blankets," he said. "You can go back to sleep."

"I am not sleepy."

"Yeah?" he said. "Well, if I go to sleep, I'm sure you'll follow."

She tugged at her braid and fell silent again.

She looked small and young and miserable.

Matt felt bad for snapping at her, so he tried to change the subject. "Hey, you know what they call these raids?"

"Raids have a name?"

"Well, last year the Germans bombed London, right?"

"That was called 'the Blitz,'" Rachel said, though she pronounced it "bleetz."

"That's right. They dropped bombs on London every single day for three months. They destroyed a third of the city." Matt stopped at the column where they'd been earlier. "Well, the Brits started hitting back."

"Like Eric," she said. "Fighting the Japanese."

"Yeah, like Eric. So the Germans switched to these air raids in reprisal. In, um, payback. They call this the 'Baedeker Blitz.'"

Rachel wrinkled her nose. "What is a baydecker?"

"Baedeker. They're guidebooks, I guess. Like travel guides?"

"The Germans want to stop travel?"

"No, they want to break the Brits' spirits. They're targeting important buildings. Historical sites, things like that. The Nazis said they're going to bomb every city with a three-star rating in the Baedeker guides."

"And Canterbury has three stars?"

"We've got five," Matt told her, even though he wasn't sure if it was true. Still, he figured if they were getting bombed, they deserved as many stars as possible.

He spread the blankets beside the wall behind a column, in a quiet nook. He sat beside Rachel and patted the floor. "Down, Chief."

Instead of lying beside Matt, Chief nuzzled Rachel, then laid down beside *her*. Like he didn't even remember whose dog he was.

Matt scowled to himself and lifted the woolen hunting cap to his nose. It smelled of his father and of his *real* home, back in the States. Wood smoke and snowfall and pipe tobacco. With his father always working and Eric on a boat in the Pacific, Matt was trying to be the man of the family.

He didn't feel grown-up, though. He just felt tired and cranky and scared. All he wanted to do was curl up and cry. And the bombs hadn't even started falling around the shelter.

At least not yet.

CHAPTER 7

The girl-pup's breathing turned quieter. She wasn't asleep, but she was resting. Her skinny arm draped across Chief's shoulder. Meanwhile, the boy-pup watched his mother on the other side of the stone cave.

Chief saw Matt's sadness as clear as if the boy-pup had a tail to put between his legs. He was scared, and he wanted to be with his parents. But his father wasn't here, and his mother was helping a woman who would give birth to a human pup.

Chief knew that a newborn would come soon.

Not yet, though. He flared his nostrils and smelled sweat and soap in the stone cave. He smelled the scents of a hundred houses clinging to the clothing of the humans.

He smelled ash too. He heard the growl of the iron birds in the sky, dropping more fire-rocks on the city.

Voices echoed and crashed in the stone cave, but through the clamor, Chief heard a familiar patter of footsteps. He cocked his head to locate the sound.

There, at the entrance!

The father was entering the stone cave.

Chief woofed softly at Matt, and twisted his ears to show where he was listening.

"Dad!" Matt yipped, and scrambled to his feet.

Matt ran across the stone cave toward the father. Chief felt the boy-pup's gladness . . . then noticed how the father was standing. His shoulders were slumped, his head was down. He looked like he was suffering, even though Chief didn't smell any blood.

Chief's ears flattened. Something was wrong with the father.

The girl-pup noticed too. She whined and followed the boy toward the old ones. Her head-tail bobbed between her shoulders.

Chief slunk along behind her and Matt. Before they reached the old ones, the father hugged the mother and started crying.

"They sent the telegram to me at work," the father said. "It's Eric."

Chief's ears pricked at the sound "Eric" and at the grief in the father's voice. Something was *very* wrong.

"Oh no," the mother whimpered. "No, no."

The humans whimpered softly to each other. The mother stank of misery, of hopelessness.

"What?" Matt asked, stopping short. "What's wrong?"

His father made a noise like a wounded animal, and his mother knelt and took both her pups in her arms. She stroked their heads and talked quietly to them. Matt started shivering.

Chief whined and licked his hand.

Rachel smelled confused. She didn't understand what was wrong. She cried, though, feeling the mother's and father's fear and sorrow.

Chief heard the sound "Eric" again, and he made himself stay near the pups even though he wanted to pace, he wanted to prowl, he wanted to *hunt*. Something was wrong with the pack: he needed to find the threat and stop it.

But this wasn't the kind of threat you could sink your teeth into. This was worse. This was grief and loss. So Chief wedged himself between Rachel and Matt, so they could lean on him if they needed to.

Matt didn't lean. Instead, he wiped tears from his face and straightened up. His long-paws tightened into fists, and his fear turned into a blaze of anger.

"It's your fault!" he shouted at his parents. "You could've stopped him. You didn't have to let him go. It's *your* fault Eric is gone!"

The boy howled and snarled and ran away.

Chief's muscles bunched with urgency. He wanted to stay with the grieving pack—with Rachel and the old ones. But he *needed* to follow Matt. He needed to protect him!

CHAPTER 8

12:45 A.M.

Matt staggered across the crypt. Faces turned toward him. Arms reached for him. The clamor of hundreds of people pounded in his head.

Columns rose like stone guards. His eyes blurred with tears.

MISSING IN ACTION.

That's what the telegram had said.

THE SECRETARY OF WAR DESIRES

ME TO EXPRESS HIS DEEP REGRET
THAT YOUR SON, MARINE PRIVATE
ERIC DAWSON, HAS BEEN REPORTED
MISSING IN ACTION . . .

Eric was MIA. Missing in action.

Gone.

Vanished.

Matt stumbled and almost fell. He caught himself on the wall and just stood there, his forehead against the cool stone.

Eric was okay. He had to be. They'd find him again.

He was just missing. Not KIA. Not killed in action.

Missing.

Tears leaked out of Matt's eyes. He heard the *click-clack* of Chief's nails on the floor behind him and felt Chief's snout nuzzling his hand.

He couldn't even stand to look at Chief, not now. Chief didn't know what was happening. He didn't know the world was at war. He didn't know they were hiding from bombs. He didn't know Eric was gone.

The room spun around Matt. He couldn't take it. He couldn't just stand around in a crypt while Eric was missing somewhere in the Pacific, halfway around the world.

He needed to be alone.

Matt heard his father call his name, and he lurched toward an alcove in the shadows, away from the hustle and bustle of the main room. The alcove was dark and cool, but Matt's anger suddenly burned as bright and hot as an incendiary bomb.

"He didn't have to go!" Matt muttered, his voice echoing against the stone. "Not so soon. Why did he go? Why did they *let* him?"

If only Eric hadn't enlisted, he'd still be safe. They'd still be together. And—and even if he'd enlisted later, at least he wouldn't be MIA now.

Instead, he'd left Mom and Dad behind.

He'd left *Matt* behind.

Eyes stinging with tears, Matt stumbled into a flight of stairs. He kept running, like he was trying to escape the news, and found himself in a narrow stone hallway. Through a window, he saw the yellow-and-orange light of the Germans' glowing flares reflecting against the branches of a tree.

Then he caught sight of pale, stern faces staring down at him.

Cold, unforgiving faces. His heart clenched, and he jerked backward—then realized that the faces were just cathedral statues.

He took a slow breath . . . and heard a rumbling buzz. As he cocked his head, the noise turned into a mechanical growl—it was the German bombers, louder than before!

And closer than ever. They were directly overhead!

Matt panicked. He spun back toward the air-raid shelter, but when he squeezed through the door, the smell of dirt surrounded him. He'd run in the wrong direction!

He darted into the closest stairway and ran up a flight of stone stairs to a wide balcony.

He wasn't trying to reach the shelter anymore. He wasn't trying to escape the danger. He was trying to escape from that moment when his father had showed him the telegram.

Matt skidded to a halt in a chapel with rows

of stained-glass windows. He slumped against the wall, then slid down to the floor and pulled his knees to his chest.

Eric was still alive. Matt knew he was. He was probably washed ashore on a deserted Pacific island, building an SOS signal on the beach with rocks or logs. One day soon Matt would see him again, and they'd play ball and eat ice cream.

Matt squeezed his eyes shut. When he'd been six or seven years old, Eric had taken him to buy ice-cream cones on a hot summer day. The top scoop of Matt's cone fell off and smeared down his shirt. He'd cried. So Eric had given Matt his shirt, which was so big it fell to Matt's calves like a baggy dress. He hadn't cared that he'd looked silly. He'd been so proud to wear Eric's shirt he hadn't even minded dropping his ice cream.

Opening his eyes, Matt took a shaky breath. He needed to be strong. Eric would be fine. And Eric made Matt promise to take care of Chief, so that's exactly what he'd do.

Which meant he needed to get back to the shelter.

He rose unsteadily—and the *click-clack* of

claws on the stone floor almost made him laugh. He didn't need to find Chief. Chief had found him!

"Chief!" he called. "I'm in here!"

The *click-clack* came faster as Chief trotted closer. He barked twice, sharp warning barks, and started to run.

Matt felt a jolt of panic at the warning barks. Something was wrong! He started toward Chief and—

A bomb exploded outside.

The stained-glass windows shattered, and the surge of air felt like a slap on Matt's face. The sound deafened him. His fear made his knees buckle, and the blast slammed him to the ground.

Billows of dust blinded Matt, and an ache pounded in his head. He couldn't hear Chief anymore; he couldn't hear his own gasps and whimpers. He couldn't hear anything at all.

CHAPTER 9

When Matt ran into the corner of the stone cave, Chief hesitated beside the girl-pup and the old ones.

At least until he realized that the boy-pup *wasn't* in the corner. He'd left the cave through a different tunnel.

He was gone.

Chief broke free of the pack and dashed across the cave. He smelled a whiff of perfume, the tang of tears. He heard a wheezing breath, the crinkle of paper, the shuffle of a shoe against the floor.

He caught Matt's trail.

It led into a stairway. Chief followed, loping higher until he lost the scent in the overwhelming smell of freshly dug earth.

Chief put his nose to the ground. He ran in one direction, then the other.

There! He found the trail again and heard the iron birds flying closer in the sky. He heard the whistle of fire-rocks falling.

He ran toward Matt and scrambled around a corner, slipping on the smooth stone. He heard the boy-pup's breathing and smelled the salty damp of his sadness.

Matt yelled the sound that meant he needed help: "Chief!"

Chief ran closer, trying to reach Matt before the fire-rock hit the ground. He knew he couldn't win the race, but that didn't matter. The pup needed him. Muscles straining, he sped forward . . .

The fire-rock boomed.

The blast lifted Chief like a pair of massive jaws grabbing the scruff of his neck. It shook him and tossed him across the room. Glass fell and

shattered across the floor with tiny sharp teeth.

Chief crashed into a wooden bench and slumped limply.

His vision turned black—but he woke suddenly moments later. Maybe moments. He couldn't tell. The glass wasn't falling anymore. The iron bird was flying away, getting quieter.

And Matt was gone.

Still disoriented by the blast, Chief inhaled deeply. He needed to find the boy-pup, but a thousand new scents swirled in the air: scorched cloth and charred leaves and melting rubber.

Which way had the boy-pup run?

Either outside into the night, or higher in the old building. Surely even a human wasn't foolish enough to run higher, toward the iron birds!

Except Chief knew that humans didn't have any sense. That's why they needed dogs to look after them.

So he prowled carefully closer, sniffing deeply, alert for the slightest hint of Matt.

And a familiar smell tugged at him!

He turned suddenly and ran through the wreckage toward the door leading to the lawn.

Just there, in the doorway, he found the woolen hat that smelled of the father, of the older boy, of the pregnant woman—and of Matt. He must've come this way.

When Chief ran outside, the trail ended in the stink of the burning city: charred cloth and blistered paint. He growled in frustration, his ears pricking for the sound of Matt's voice, for his footsteps. Too many noises!

Maybe the boy-pup had run back to the den. The house. Chief would look for him there. And if he didn't find him?

He'd keep looking. When a pack member was in trouble, you never gave up.

CHAPTER 10

Matt's hearing returned with a low, aching hum. He scrambled to his feet, trembling. His ears hurt and his head pounded and—and where was Chief?

He must have been caught in the blast!

Still shaking, Matt took a breath and called, "Chief?"

He peered through the smoke and dust. He didn't see Chief anywhere. He whistled and called again but still didn't hear anything.

Then he saw the stairway leading upward. *Oh no.*

"Here, boy!" he called.

The stupid dog must've gotten spooked by the explosion and bolted upstairs.

Matt blinked at the stairway. He knew he should run for the shelter, but he wasn't about to lose Chief. He'd promised to look after Eric's dog, and that's exactly what he'd do.

So he took a deep breath and started toward the stairway.

Halfway there, he realized that he'd lost his father's woolen hat in the explosion. No time to look for it now, though. It didn't matter.

He started up the stairs. The stone was uneven, worn from centuries of use—and slippery. Matt almost fell twice before he reached the first door. He almost grabbed the knob, but realized that didn't make sense.

Chief was a smart dog, but not even he could operate a doorknob!

Matt climbed higher. Yellow light shone on the stone a minute before he came to an open door. The air smelled like a bonfire, and he heard men shouting roughly.

Matt peered through the door and found himself looking onto one of the cathedral's roofs. There must've been dozens of them, tucked between all the towers and spires. This one was only slightly angled, with high walls rising along two sides.

A man was standing in the open, beside a small mound on the roof. For a terrible moment, Matt thought the mound was Chief lying there.

Except no, it wasn't a dog. It was a low heap of . . . something.

Matt frowned and looked closer. He couldn't tell what it was. And what was the man *doing*? He was skinny and sort of rat-faced, and he looked suspicious to Matt. Was he making trouble? Was he working with the Germans?

Then Matt spotted two other men on the roof! What kind of people stood around on a cathedral roof during an air raid?

A knot of worry tightened in Matt's chest—then the rat-faced man glanced toward the door where he was standing.

Matt froze, afraid of being spotted. He didn't move, he didn't breathe. He focused on the sound of the wind buffeting the cathedral spires.

The rat-faced man didn't see Matt in the shadows, though.

Matt exhaled shakily. He'd tell the people in the shelter when he got back. But Chief wasn't here, so he'd keep on searching. He started to turn away, and a hand grabbed his arm.

"Yeee!" he yelped, almost jumping out of his skin.

When he spun, he didn't see a shadowy figure or a rat-faced man. No, he saw *Rachel* standing in the doorway. Following him, like always!

"Would you get lost!" he snapped at her.

"Oi!" a man shouted from the roof. "What're you kids doing?"

Matt turned back and found Rat Face staring at him, holding a big net. Big enough to catch a kid.

"Don't move!" the man snarled at them.

"I, um, we're looking for—" Matt couldn't say

"my dog!" "Um, the shelter! Sorry, bye!"

Rat Face took a step toward them. He started to say something . . . then stopped at a loud *CLATTER*. Something hard had slammed into the roof and now skittered through the shadows.

"A bomb!" Rachel gasped.

She was right. The German planes were trying to bomb the cathedral, and they'd dropped an incendiary—a firebomb—only twenty feet away. But it hadn't exploded. Not yet. Matt knew that some incendiary bombs didn't burst into flames immediately. Instead, it took a few seconds for the chemicals inside to mix together and ignite after dropping.

Only a few seconds, though! Matt stared in horror, waiting for the bomb to explode.

Instead, it rolled to a halt ten feet away—and Rat Face sprang into action.

He ran *toward* the bomb and threw his net on it.

Except it wasn't a net. It was a big square of burlap. That's what the heap was made of: burlap sacks, for handling bombs!

Matt's knees trembled. One second passed. Two seconds! He knew that inside the firebomb, the chemicals must be mixing together. He knew the bomb was about burst into superhot flames.

Still, Rat Face didn't falter. He grabbed the bomb with the burlap.

He raced to the side of the roof.

He threw the bomb off the cathedral.

A moment later, the bomb hit the grass—and burst into flames.

The fire blazed brightly, scorching the lawn, but it didn't burn the building. That's what the men were doing on the roof! They were fire-watchers, catching bombs before they ignited and throwing them over the edge.

Matt gazed in amazement at the man—and another bomb fell.

It clattered and rolled . . . and stopped between the man and the pile of burlap.

He wouldn't have time to run for another cloth. The bomb would start the cathedral burning!

Without pausing to think, Matt raced to the heap of burlap. He grabbed the top sheet and

whipped around toward Rat Face. How long before the bomb exploded? The other one had only taken a few seconds. How much time did Matt have left?

CHAPTER 11

The man on the roof yelled at Matt. He probably swore too, but Matt didn't hear the words.

With his heart beating fast enough to burst from his chest, Matt raced across the roof.

He stretched toward the man. The man snatched the burlap from Matt, shoved him toward the door, and darted at the bomb.

Matt stumbled. He looked over his shoulder once before he reached the door and caught a glimpse of the man standing at the edge of the roof, heaving the bomb into the darkness.

Flames glowed behind the firewatcher, and Matt didn't know how he'd ever thought the man looked rat-faced. At that moment he looked exactly like a movie hero or a monument of bravery.

Then Rachel grabbed Matt's hand and tugged him into the cathedral stairwell.

"We need to get back to the shelter," Matt said.

"Vee can't," Rachel told him, her accent thicker from fear. "Not yet."

"Of course we can! We need to—"

"I saw Chief," she said, "running into the city."

"Oh no!" Matt thought for a second as they clattered down the stairs. "You go back to the shelter. I'll find him."

Rachel didn't say anything. She just looked at him.

"C'mon, Rachel. *Please.*" Matt couldn't look after her and Chief at the same time. "Please go back to Mom and Dad."

She still didn't say anything. She was going to

tag along like always, and he couldn't stop her. He wanted to yell at her, but he knew that wouldn't help.

"Fine!" he blurted, exasperated. "Come with me then. Just . . . be careful."

She nodded and continued down the stairs. Matt followed her to the ground floor of the cathedral and then outside. They headed along a walkway with arches open to the night.

"Wait a second," Matt said, and listened for planes.

He didn't want anyone to throw a bomb off the cathedral roof, straight onto their heads. He didn't hear anything, though. He'd read that bombers came in waves—first one squadron of bombers, then a pause, then another squadron.

Maybe this was the quiet period between two waves. He knew the raid wasn't over completely; the sirens hadn't sounded the "all clear" yet.

He and Rachel ran across the lawn, darted past a tree with a huge knobby trunk—then stopped short. Matt gasped, and Rachel blurted something in Yiddish when they saw the city spread out at the bottom of the hill.

Entire streets were engulfed in flames. Tiny figures were silhouetted against the flames. A few cars rolled through the rubble-strewn streets, barely visible in the light of the fires. A single fire truck stood in a crossroads.

Matt swallowed. "Chief's down there somewhere. We—someone's going to come looking for us soon, to take us back to the shelter. We have to find Chief first!"

"Then we find him."

"Which way was he running?"

She pointed. "There, I think."

"Let's go." Matt started away. "Stay close."

To his surprise, Rachel actually giggled.

He didn't understand for a second, then he laughed. He was always yelling at her for following him, and now he wanted her to stay close.

They ran downhill, calling for Chief.

The poor dog. He needed Matt. How could a dog survive an air raid? Chief must be so confused and afraid. He didn't understand what was happening. He didn't know how to take care of himself.

The street was empty at first. Flames glowed

over the rooftops. An engine sounded, and Rachel's grip tightened on Matt's hand.

He pulled her into a doorframe for protection, but the engine wasn't a plane. It was a car. A dark-green sedan with a big grille and a woman behind the wheel.

"Oh!" he said. "She's ATS."

Rachel tugged on her braid. "Eighty what?"

"ATS," he said more clearly. "The women's branch of the British army."

The car rumbled over a scattering of bricks in the road, thrown there after a bomb struck a nearby wall.

"They are ambulance," Rachel said.

"Nah," Matt told her. "Ambulances are bigger and—" He stopped when he saw another woman in the back seat, helping an injured man. "Oh! You're right."

"Little ambulance," Rachel said.

"Yeah. I guess they're evacuating the wounded in staff cars." He realized that Rachel wouldn't know what that meant. "Er, which are officers' cars. Those ladies are the drivers."

"The wounded?" Rachel said, her eyes

widening. She didn't care about the cars, she cared about the people!

"Don't worry," Matt told her as the car rolled around the corner. "I'm sure we won't run across any trouble."

"Okay, if you are sure." She grabbed his arm. "Do you hear?"

"Hear what? The sirens? The bombers? The—"

"Hush!" she said.

He thought she was being silly, but he pretended to listen for a second. And that's when he heard it: a faint cry sounding from behind a half-fallen brick wall.

A quiet plea for help.

CHAPTER 12

1:11 A.M.

Chief prowled through ash-filled, rubble-strewn streets. The boy-pup needed him. How could a *human* survive all this trouble? Matt must be so confused and afraid. He didn't understand what was happening. He didn't know how to take care of himself.

The smoke stung Chief's eyes and clogged his nostrils. Too many scents. Burning wood, burning fabric. The greasy stench of charred rubber.

The crackle of the flames and the crumble of the buildings sounded louder now than everything except the sirens.

Chief slunk along the sidewalk outside the house. Faint scent trails branched from the front door. Old trails, but where was the boy-pup *now*?

A truck drove past. Chief watched carefully, then trotted toward the center of the city, the place most crowded with buildings.

Humans shouted and barked in the distance. Chief prowled along a street where flames crawled through the walls of the buildings. Maybe the boy-pup was with the other humans?

Chief didn't smell him, though. He didn't hear his voice.

He listened closely, and he heard something else. A few of the men *sounded* like his family. Their growls and barks reminded him of the way Matt and the old ones spoke—and mostly of Eric, the one who'd raised Chief.

They sounded familiar. They sounded like puppyhood, like home.

Chief trotted toward them. Ash fell like snow onto his fur. Hoses spread across the street like giant snakes as men sprayed water on the fires. Filthy puddles formed on the ground.

The two men with the familiar voices jogged toward the fire truck. "We've got to help the Brits!" one of them said.

"Remember what you told me before we went on leave?" the other man grumped. "'Let's visit Canterbury, it'll be relaxing . . .'"

"Hey, buddy!" the first man called to the firemen. "We're here to help. What do you need?"

"You're Americans?"

"That's right, US Army," the first man said. "We're on leave, but tell us what you need and we'll get to work."

"We're clearing houses. Ensuring nobody's still inside." The fireman gestured to a few houses. "See that lot? They've already been cleared. You two start at that door there."

Chief didn't understand the words or smell the boy-pup . . . but he did hear a faint scratching. A *scrrt, scrrt, scrrt* sounded through the clamor.

The noise came from a house with smoke billowing from the windows. *Scrrt, scrrt, scrrt.* Someone was alive in there.

Someone needed help.

Chief dashed forward, though the smoke. Past

a metal box. Over the hoses. Along the sidewalk. His eyes watered, and his nose burned. Embers fell on his back and charred his fur.

"What's that dog doing?" someone yelled. "He's running into the fire!"

"You, Yanks! Stop him!"

One of the men loomed in front of Chief. "C'mere, boy!"

Chief stopped. The man sounded *very* familiar. Just like Eric.

"C'mon, boy! We're the United States Army! If you can't trust us, who can you trust?"

Chief eyed the man, but his ears still swiveled, tracking the scratching coming from inside the burning house. *Scrrt, scrrt, scrrt.*

"He hears something inside!" the familiar-sounding man called.

"That house is clear!" another man shouted back.

"Okay, I'll grab him." The familiar man reached for Chief, but Chief easily pranced away. Humans were so slow. "Stay!" the man shouted at him. "Sit!"

Chief waited for the man to crouch down,

then raced past him and sped toward the fire.

He burst through the open door. Smoke burned his eyes. *Scrrt, scrrt, scrrt.* He scrambled into a room with little desks. Bright flames climbed one wall. The heat stung his nose, and he stayed close to a high counter that blocked the fire.

The scratching sounded louder.

Chief dashed into a back room. A heavy beam had fallen from the ceiling and smashed a row of cabinets. Wood paneling and metal bits scattered the floor.

In the middle of the wreckage, a narrow table was bowed under the weight of the beam. The remains of a broken cabinet surrounded it. But where was the person?

Scrrt, scrrt, scrrt. The scratching was coming from under the table!

Chief started digging at the smashed cabinet that was trapping the person beneath the table.

He didn't flinch from the heat or the embers scorching his ears and nose. He didn't smell the stinging fumes. He didn't notice the shattered glass jabbing his paws.

He just dug toward the *scrrt, scrrt, scrrt*.

"Hello?" a wavering voice said from under the table. "Is someone there?"

Chief barked and dug faster.

"I hear him!" the familiar voice called from inside the house. "Come here, boy! *Come*! Get out of there!"

Chief barked again. Smoke filled his lungs, but he didn't stop digging. He'd never stop digging, not while he still heard that *scrrt, scrrt, scrrt*.

The familiar man ran into the kitchen. "You stupid mutt, get your shaggy—"

"Hello?" the voice called from under the table.

"Holy Moses!" The man stopped in shock, then bellowed, "There's someone trapped! Get in here!"

The man crouched beside Chief, tugging at the shattered cupboard. He pulled and heaved as Chief dug. The cabinet shifted two inches, three inches . . .

More men ran into the back room. The humans yelped at each other, but Chief didn't listen. He kept digging, panting for breath in the smoke-filled room.

Crash!

The cupboard tore free. Two of the men crawled under the table and helped a fur-faced human onto his feet.

"Your dog . . ." The fur-faced human gasped, reaching toward Chief. "He saved me."

Chief raised his head to lick the man's hand . . . then staggered. The smoke seemed to squeeze the air from his lungs.

He panted faster but couldn't catch his breath. He felt weak and dizzy. He curled his tail under his belly, and his vision darkened.

CHAPTER 13

Matt darted closer to the half-fallen wall. He paused, listening for the cry for help.

"Can you hear anything?" he asked Rachel.

"I think it came from that way," she said, pointing past the wall.

They jogged to a cobbled drive that led into a dark courtyard. One half of the courtyard must've been a lawn before the war, but it was a vegetable garden now.

"Help!" the voice called again.

Matt jogged through the smoke and darkness,

and he spotted an old woman kneeling beside an old man who was lying on the ground.

For a terrible moment, Matt thought the man was dead. But no, he was holding the woman's hand tight.

"What happened?" Matt flushed for asking such a stupid question. He knew what happened; they got caught in an air raid! "I mean, do you need help?"

"Children!" the old woman snapped. "Get to a shelter at once!"

Matt and Rachel looked at each other. Matt knew that Rachel was thinking the same thing he was; they couldn't just leave this old couple lying here in the open.

"We will," he told her. "But we'll send help on the way."

Rachel looked at the old man. "Is he okay?"

"I'm afraid my husband can't move his leg," the old woman said, her voice sharp with fear. "However, you children have no such excuse, and must—"

Crrrrrk-slam!

Somewhere out of eyeshot, a roof collapsed.

Over the rooftops, dust and smoke swirled into the air. The fire glowed yellow on the clouds of ash. Matt looked toward the cathedral but couldn't see anything through all the smoke. He hoped his parents were okay.

"Little ambulance?" Rachel asked Matt.

"Definitely." He gazed around the dark courtyard. "Which way was it going?"

Rachel pointed. "Toward St. George Street. Toward the fire."

"Okay. You stay here in case they need anything, I'll run for the ATS ladies." Except he'd only taken three steps when he heard Rachel following him. He spun around. "Stay here!"

She shook her head.

"Would you listen to me for once?"

She tugged on her braid. "We stick together."

"Your sister's a good girl," the wounded man groaned. "Looking after her brother like that."

Matt scowled. The man thought *Rachel* was looking after *him*? He didn't say anything, though, because he was pretty sure you weren't supposed to yell at injured old men. He just jogged away, toward St. George Street.

Toward the fire.

"You've got to do what I say," he told Rachel. "We're in the middle of an air raid!"

"I will. I promise. If you say, I will do."

"So when I tell you to stay put, *stay put.*"

"Except not staying put."

"Rachel!" he snapped as they jogged along the middle of the street. "That's the only thing I need from you!"

She didn't say anything until they paused at the corner. "Would you stay put if Eric told you?"

"*Yes,*" Matt said. "Of course!"

"Oh," she said.

"So?"

"So in that case," she said. "I still will not."

"This isn't a game, Rachel! I'm not just being mean or—"

"There!" She pointed. "Ambulance!"

Hooded headlights cast dim light on the rubble-strewn street. A dark green sedan prowled into view. A massive dent on the hood caught the flickering flames, and scratches crisscrossed the car roof: it must've been hit by falling debris.

A young ATS woman sat behind the wheel,

but not the same one they'd seen earlier. There must've been a bunch of them driving down the dark, deadly streets, ferrying the wounded to the hospital.

Matt and Rachel waved their arms until the sedan stopped. "There's an old man!" Matt blurted. "He's got a broken leg or something!"

"Where's your mum?" the woman in the passenger seat asked. "Have you a shelter at home?"

"No, but we, um—"

"Vee saw the old man!" Rachel interrupted, her accent thickening. "He can't shake his leg."

The ATS woman blinked at her. "Pardon?"

"He's back that way," Matt said. "He needs help."

The ATS women looked at each other, then one said, "We'll find him. You run along to the nearest shelter. And take your sister."

"There's a shelter in the school," the other women told him. "You know where that is?"

Matt shook his head. "I'm not sure."

"I know," Rachel said, taking Matt's hand to lead him.

When the car started to drive off, Matt ran

alongside and shouted, "Wait, wait!"

The car slowed, and the driver looked through the window. "What's wrong?"

"Have you seen a dog? A big dog, running around lost?"

"Tonight? I can't imagine that any—" The sound of gunfire tore through the night, and the driver quieted.

"Oh no," Matt said, his stomach sinking as he looked again toward the smoke-obscured cathedral.

"That sound is good news, lad." The driver gave a satisfied grunt. "That's our boys! That's antiaircraft fire, taking the fight to the Nazis."

"And bad news as well," the other ATS woman said. "If they're firing, there's another wave of bombers on the way."

Sure enough, Matt heard the distant drone of bombers. His skin crawled, and Rachel muttered in Yiddish.

"Run to the shelter!" the ATS driver said. "Now! Hurry!"

CHAPTER 14

1:30 A.M.

Matt and Rachel rounded the corner at a run. The sky was gone. The moon and stars were gone. Nothing was visible overhead but the smoke that covered Canterbury, swallowing up even the cathedral steeple.

And the growl of the bombers sounded louder and louder!

"More planes!" Rachel said.

"Maybe that's just the roar of the fire," Matt said. "Or—or fire trucks."

"No." Rachel grabbed his hand. "More planes."

"Which way is the school?"

"Here," she said, pulling him along the sidewalk.

"I hope they've got a basement," he said. "Or a—"

The *BOOM* of a high-explosive bomb shattered the night.

Rubble spewed into the street from the end of the block. Windows shattered, walls burst. Twists of blackened metal pinged against cobblestones, and bits of charred cloth drifted in the air.

Rachel stumbled, shouting in fear.

Matt pulled her to her feet. His skin prickled with fear. His throat closed. The whistle of a falling bomb screeched in his ears.

He couldn't move. He couldn't think. All he could do was stand there holding Rachel's hand while she shivered and—

No! No, his sister needed him.

He needed to be strong for her, like Eric would've been for him.

He dragged Rachel backward. Glowing

embers billowed around him, the sparks prickling his exposed skin like mosquito bites. A chunk of splintery wood slammed into the ground ten feet away and scraped across the cobblestones.

Without warning, another explosion sounded behind them. Matt flinched and ran faster. Faster. Dirt flew over his head and stung the back of his neck. He ran until he couldn't tell if the noise was bombs or rescue workers or the pounding of his own heart.

Finally, he turned to Rachel. "Are you okay?"

Her cheeks were pale, and her eyes were big. She said something in Polish or Yiddish, her voice faint. Still, she squeezed his hand and tried to smile.

He tried to smile back.

Neither of them did a great job, but he still felt some of his fear fade. He scrambled onward, turned a corner—and a red-faced man with wild eyes spun to face them.

"Turn yourselves around!" the man shouted in a thick English accent. "Get back, away from Butchery Lane!"

Matt stumbled backward, not understanding.

"It's a firebreak! It's burning, the whole thing—"

A firebreak? Matt remembered Eric telling him about those. A firebreak was a cleared strip of land, with no bushes or trees—or anything flammable. It was wide enough that a fire couldn't cross it.

But Butchery Lane was a street in downtown Canterbury. What did the man mean it was a firebreak? Were they letting the whole street burn to the ground, so the fire couldn't spread into the rest of the city?

Matt didn't know. He didn't ask. He just blindly led Rachel through the smoke-filled streets. She kept repeating a singsong phrase under her voice, and he realized she was praying.

Bombs fell around them. Thick smoke changed the city into a nightmare. Matt heard the clatter of a bomb and saw a blaze of intense fire. His mind raced with fear: now the Germans were dropping both incendiary bombs *and* five-hundred-pound high-explosive bombs? The

incendiaries burst into super-hot flames, but the HE bombs blasted entire buildings into rubble.

As Matt stumbled away from the flames, a bone-shaking explosion almost knocked him to the ground!

He grabbed Rachel's hand and dashed into a side street. Smoke stung his eyes, and the dark city streets spread in front of him, strange and threatening.

Finally he and Rachel stumbled into a sprawling, shadowy city park with a big mound. After a moment, Matt recognized the area. "Oh! This is the park!"

Rachel wrinkled her nose. "Which park?"

"Where I tried to teach you baseball."

"The baseball is silly," Rachel said. She hadn't hit a single ball. She could barely hold the bat right.

Matt's fear faded a little at the familiar surroundings. He turned in a circle, getting his bearings. According to Eric, this had been a Roman cemetery almost two thousand years earlier. The old city walls ran along one side of the park. The bandstand had been torn down for scrap metal to help with the war, and some kind of military warehouse was dug into the wall nearby. Not a shelter, though. They still needed the school for that.

Now that he'd stopped running, Matt realized that he'd been hearing a rhythmic pounding for a while.

"I guess that's antiaircraft fire," he told Rachel. "Like the ATS woman said."

"Oh no," Rachel said. "More fire?"

"No, no! It's a good thing! It's the Brits shooting back at the bombers."

"The Brits," Rachel repeated, because she thought it was funny that the British were called "Brits" and the Americans were called "Yanks."

"That's right," he said, looking at the smoke-filled sky. "And do you hear that?"

"I hear a lot of *thats*."

"That new engine sound! I bet it's RAF night fighters finally come to blast a few holes in Jerry!"

"British fighter planes?"

"Yeah." Matt glanced down at Rachel. "They'll teach Fritz a lesson."

Rachel squeezed his hand and shot him a

quick, grateful look. She knew he was trying to distract her by using the terms "Jerry" and "Fritz" for the Germans.

"Now, um . . ." He frowned. "Which way is the school?"

Rachel pointed across the dark garden. "I think there."

"Okay, we'll run on three," Matt said. "You count."

Rachel nodded as Matt gripped her hand. "One, two . . . three!"

They raced from the park onto the street. As they ran toward the west, the glow of the fire got farther away. The sound of explosions sounded fainter, too, along with the shouting and sirens.

Matt exhaled in relief. Finally, they were getting away from the target area. But what about Chief? What about his parents? Were they still in the cathedral? If he knew them, they'd be on the streets looking for him and Rachel.

A car rolled through an intersection ahead of them, as more ATS women searched for the wounded. Two fire trucks with hooded lights sped along Castle Street behind them.

"I bet they're from other towns," Matt told Rachel. "Coming to help fight the fires."

Rachel tugged on her braid. "I'm a little twisted around."

"A little what?"

"Twisted around. I forget which way is the school."

"Oh!" he said. "You're a little *turned* around."

"No, I'm not!" she announced with a sudden smile. "Is this way!"

She jogged along the street, toward the school and Greyfriars gardens. Matt liked Greyfriars. He liked wandering along the narrow canal and walking the meandering paths. And he liked the view of the cathedral spires.

Matt peered at the sky above the rooftops, hoping to catch sight of the cathedral now. But he couldn't see any towers or spires through the smoke. He hoped his mom and dad were okay. He hoped that Chief had found his way back to them.

He must've. He was a smart dog. He was Eric's dog, and . . .

A wave of grief washed over him just as

suddenly as a wave of bombers. Matt didn't want to think about Eric.

He lowered his teary gaze—but not before spotting a dark shape swooping over the city.

His head sprung upward. "Look! There!"

"What?" Rachel asked. "I don't see."

The dark shape swirled and vanished over the rooftops, falling away from the burning streets, toward Greyfriars. "There was a . . . I don't know."

"Is only a few blocks to the school."

"I think it was a parachute!"

"You think from one of the English night fighters?"

Excitement kindled in Matt's heart. After running away from danger all night to save themselves, maybe they could finally run *toward* something, to help someone else. Maybe that's how Eric had felt about enlisting.

"I bet!" he told Rachel. "The pilot must've bailed out."

Rachel wrinkled her nose. "Like a bale of hay?"

"No, no! He must've parachuted out of the plane!" He grabbed Rachel's arm. "Come on, we've got to find him. We've got to check that he's okay!"

A cloud of smoke wafted down the street. Matt coughed and closed his stinging eyes—but only for a second. Then he started tugging Rachel through the choking smoke, tracking the dark shape toward where it must've fallen a few blocks away.

CHAPTER 15

In the smoke-filled back room, Chief's head spun. He struggled for breath as his vision grew darker. He smelled the bittersweet seep of gas and heard a snakelike hiss.

He whimpered a warning to the men carrying the fur-faced man away—then an explosion in a nearby room shook the walls.

Shelves cascaded onto the floor, and Chief collapsed amid the wreckage. He struggled for breath. He tried to rise onto his paws—and felt himself lifted into the arms of the first man, the one with the familiar voice.

The man smelled of sweat and countryside, with a hint of the tangy, metallic scent of blood. Chief forced his eyes open and saw ash smudging the man's face and a scratch bleeding on his cheek.

Still dizzy and weak, Chief licked the man's cut. Humans weren't very good at licking their wounds, so you needed to take care of that for them.

On the other paw, they were extremely good at carrying a dog out of a fiery building. The man brought him down the hallway, into the blast of heat and the glow of flames. Then the man staggered with him across the rubble-strewn floor, through the door. Onto the cool, wide-open street.

Fresh air filled Chief's lungs. He coughed, then struggled in the man's arms. He needed to feel the ground under his paws, to make sure he was okay.

"Is that better, boy?" the man asked, setting him on the pavement and kneeling in front of him.

Chief shook himself to chase the stink of smoke out of his fur. He tensed his shoulder muscles, he felt the strength in his legs. Much better.

"You look okay. What's your name, boy?" The man reached for the jingling collar that Chief wore to help his people find him. "Chief?"

Chief barked.

"Good boy, Chief," the man said, laying a gentle hand on his chest. "What a good boy."

"Hey, Landry," another man said. "You coming?"

"Not without Chief," the one called Landry said. "This dog's a natural."

An ominous grinding sounded from the building. Chief raised his hackles. The walls weren't going to stand for much longer.

"A natural what? Flea motel?"

"A natural search and rescue dog," Landry said.

Chief shifted impatiently. Landry kept yelping at his packmate like he couldn't tell that the building was about to collapse. Chief heard a deep creaking, then the crack of fire-weakened beams.

In a few heartbeats, the entire place would fall—and the humans were standing directly outside it, without a care in the world!

So Chief grabbed Landry's wrist in his teeth and backed him farther away.

"He's biting you!"

"He's not biting me. A German shepherd like this? If he bit me, he'd break my bones. No, he wants to show me something down the street." Landry's tone changed. "Don't you, Chief? Isn't that right?"

Chief pulled him another few steps.

"What is it, boy? What do you—"

With a *RUMBLE-CRASH*, the burning house fell in on itself. Flames washed onto the street. A wall toppled, shattering into a spray of rubble. A dust cloud rose around Chief and the men, who shouted and—finally!—ran from the danger.

"Well don't that beat all," the other man said, after they stopped down the block. "Maybe he *is* a natural."

"He's a whiz," Landry said, patting Chief's flank. "This dog is genuine army material."

Chief heard admiration in the man's smoke-roughened voice and peered up at his face. Maybe he wasn't smart enough to run from a collapsing building, but Chief liked him.

He reminded Chief of Eric.

CHAPTER 16

Matt and Rachel raced to the end of the street, chasing the fallen parachute. They clambered over a cement ridge that rose a few inches from the ground. The iron fence posts once planted in the cement had been removed for the war effort.

Grass grew on the other side of the ridge. A stone's throw in front of Matt, a few trees lofted overhead.

The air smelled of fresh water. The river ran along the base of those trees. It wasn't much of a river, actually. It was more of a canal, running smoothly between high walls. Matt liked it better than a regular, wide, unwalled river; it was more historical, almost like a moat.

"Do you see him?" Rachel asked.

Matt scanned the sky. "No."

"You are sure it was a parachute?"

"Either that or the biggest bat in the world." He followed a path closer to the river. "I guess it could've been the shadow of a plane in the smoke."

Rachel shivered. "There is no light to make shadow."

"Are you cold?" He looked at her, wrapping her arms around herself in her thin pajamas and slippers. "You look cold."

"You look cold too. I'm not going away!"

"I never said—"

"Hush," Rachel said.

"You hush!" Matt said.

"No, hush and *listen*. Do you hear that?"

"Hear what?" Matt cocked his head. *Flup. Flup-flup-flup.* "Oh! Something's flapping."

"Like a parachute?" Rachel asked.

Matt squinted into the darkness of the park. "Yeah."

"Or like the biggest bat in the world?"

"Let's find out," Matt said, and jogged toward the sound.

When he rounded a bush, he almost couldn't believe his eyes. He was right! A dark, ragged shape stretched overhead, tangled in the branches of a tree.

A black, flapping shape.

A parachute!

Cords and ropes stretched from the tree, across the ground, then disappeared.

What? That didn't make any sense.

Matt ran closer. "Oh!" he told Rachel. "The river!"

The parachute cords disappeared into the inky blackness of the canal.

"Hello?" Matt called. "Hello?"

"Here!" a man's voice replied weakly. "In here."

"Coming!" Matt said, and scrambled to the edge of the canal.

When he looked over, he found a man dangling at the end of the parachute ropes. Blood smeared his face beneath a soft leather helmet with built-in ear protectors. The river water covered his flight suit to his shoulders.

"You—you're a night fighter!" Matt said, still amazed. "You flew a Spitfire here to defend the city!"

The half-submerged, blood-streaked man peered up at Matt. "And you are the sight for the sore eyes."

Matt almost admitted that he daydreamed about flying a Spitfire, but he remembered just in time that Spitfires weren't usually used for night fighting, anyway. Instead the Brits used "Beaufighters"—and Matt couldn't let his daydreams distract him now.

"Don't worry," he said. "We're here to help."

"Good, yes." The pilot groaned. "I could use a few helping hands."

Saying "a few helping hands" instead of "a helping hand" made Matt think of Rachel, and how she sometimes got English phrases wrong. Something was strange about the man's accent, but the British often used different words for things, like "lorry" instead of "truck" and "lift" instead of "elevator."

Matt crouched down to grab the parachute

cords. He pulled and yanked, but the pilot didn't budge. Rachel grabbed a handful of the cords behind Matt. They heaved together . . . and still couldn't pull the waterlogged man from the canal.

"He's too heavy," Matt told Rachel.

"I cannot free myself from these threads," the pilot said, his voice strained as he fought to stay above the water. "And if I slip, they will keep me from the swimming . . ."

"He'll drown," Rachel breathed.

"No, he won't," Matt said. "We won't let him."

CHAPTER 17

The parachute cords jerked in Matt's hands when the pilot shifted, trying to climb up the side of the canal. Matt braced himself and tugged. The cords didn't budge.

When he looked into the canal, he saw blood dripping into the pilot's eyes from a cut on his forehead. The tangling ropes kept him from getting a grip, and he slid deeper into the water!

"Hold on!" Matt wrapped the cords around his wrists. "Rachel, tie the other end to the tree!"

"There is too much . . . I don't know the word! Loose parts."

"Too much slack?"

She scuffled behind him. "I'll get a stick!"

"A what?"

Rachel darted away, disappearing into the shadows under the tree.

"What're you going to do with a *stick*?" Matt grunted as the parachute cord tugged at his arms. If he wasn't careful, he'd get pulled into the water too.

Rachel's voice floated from the darkness. "Tie the ropes around it."

"There's no time for that!" Matt leaned backward until he fell onto his butt. He wedged his heels against the stone lip of the canal. "Hang on!"

"I am hanging," the pilot said. "Believe me."

The parachute cords slowly pulled Matt closer to the canal. He strained with all his might and held fast. "Sorry!"

The pilot swore—but not in English.

"What—" Matt felt a chill on his skin. "What's that?"

"Er, nothing for youngster ears!"

Matt peered into the darkness. "I haven't heard your accent before."

"I am . . ." A splash sounded from the river. "Scottish."

"Oh!"

A grunt arose from the darkness. "Plus I am almost drowning."

"Yeah." Matt turned his head. "Rachel! Where are you?"

Her answer floated from the shadows. "I can't find a stick big enough."

Matt chewed his lower lip. He needed to do something fast. Something better than telling Rachel to stop looking for a stupid stick. The parachute cord dug into his wrists. His arms ached with the strain. His back burned, and his knees wobbled.

He needed Eric. He needed Chief.

He needed *help*.

The parachute cord bit into his skin. The ground chilled his legs through his pajamas. He took a breath and tried to ignore the pain.

He couldn't hold on for much longer, he couldn't—

"One minute!" Rachel said, behind him.

The cords jerked and wiggled in his grip. He dug in his heels and tightened his grip.

"Done!" Rachel finally said.

Matt glanced over his shoulder. She'd wriggled a stout branch between a bunch of the parachute cords, then spun it around. The cords had gathered together, looping around the branch. The parachute was still stuck in the tree, but now the cords had a branch shoving through them, like a reel on a fishing pole.

And as Rachel turned the branch over and over, the parachute cord looped around more tightly. When she wound the cords around the branch, it took up the slack in the ropes.

In a moment, Matt felt the cords tighten from behind him. He loosened his grip, and the pilot didn't plunge into the water.

"Hold on!" he yelled, scrambling to his feet. "We've got you!"

A faint splashing sounded from the canal.

Matt darted to Rachel, flapping his hands

to get rid of the ache. "Great job, Rachel, you smarty-pants!"

She peered at him. "I have clever underwear?"

"No, I mean—oh, forget it!"

Matt helped her spin the branch around and around, pulling the parachute cord tighter . . . and dragging the pilot from the water.

Inch by inch.

The tree branches bent toward the canal.

Twigs snapped.

The cord grew tighter, wrapping around the middle of the branch.

Pretty soon, the branch stopped spinning so easily. Matt and Rachel pulled and shoved and grunted, reeling the pilot higher.

Good!" the pilot called. "Only a little more. *Schnell, schnell!*"

Rachel gasped. "Drop him! Matt, drop him!"

"What? What's wrong?"

"Didn't you hear what he said?"

"That's just Scottish."

"It's *German*. He wasn't in a British night fighter. He was in a German bomber!"

CHAPTER 18

2 A.M.

Down the block from the collapsed house, Chief shook himself until he felt his strength return. He still stank of smoke—and of the biting scent of burned fur—but his ears were pricked and his teeth were sharp. Ready for anything.

The two men from the burning building jogged down the street ahead of him. The one named Landry snapped his fingers at Chief, which Chief knew meant that he'd need help again soon. So Chief ran alongside him, listening for trouble.

"What do you know about dogs, Landry?" the packmate said.

"My aunt's got a kennel," Landry told him. "Have you heard of the Dogs for Defense program?"

One of the men with the hoses asked, "Dogs for the fence?"

"*Defense*. Dogs for Defense."

"What's that?"

"A new program for training dogs to serve in the US military."

"Oh! You've got that thick American accent."

"I don't have an accent! You're the one with the accent."

The men barked laughter at each other like silly puppies, then pointed to various buildings and streets. The iron birds were flying closer overhead. Chief narrowed his eyes. He couldn't see through the smoke, but that didn't matter. He could track every one of the falling fire-rocks by sound alone.

"Chief!" the man named Landry said. "This way!"

Chief started to follow them—then stopped.

He'd caught scent of Matt and Rachel! He sniffed the smoky air.

"What're you smelling, boy?"

Chief inhaled again, but the scent faded. Where *were* they? A couple of furless human pups weren't safe in the fiery night, not without a dog to help them.

"Chief?"

Chief growled in frustration. He'd lost the scent. He paced back and forth for a moment, trying to find it again. It was gone, though, so he followed Landry into a block of flattened buildings where flames danced among the ruins. Puddles of water from the hoses collected between cobblestones. The stench of burning oil hurt Chief's nose.

He raised his ruff at the smell and followed along.

"Find!" Landry said to him.

Chief didn't know who "Find" was, so he watched the man.

"Find!" Landry repeated.

"What're you doing?" the other man asked. "He doesn't speak English."

"That's the word some rescue dogs are trained with," Landry said. "You play hide-and-seek with them as puppies. When they find you, you give them a treat. Over and over. Then someone else hides, and you tell them 'Find!' And you give them a treat when they find that person. It's standard training."

"Well, this one's looking at you like that Englishman. Doesn't understand a word."

"Chief," Landry said, crouching down, muzzle to muzzle. "You're a good boy."

Chief licked Landry's face again. That scratch of his needed attention.

Landry smiled. "You're the whiz around here. C'mon, boy. If you hear anything, you let me know."

Chief knew the man wanted something, but he didn't know what. Probably the man didn't know what he wanted either. Humans often didn't.

So when Landry started trotting down the street, Chief loped alongside him. Staying alert for any out-of-place smells or noises in the ruined buildings. Someone could be alive in there.

And nobody would know but him.

CHAPTER 19

Matt froze. "German? Are you sure?"

"Of course I am sure!" Rachel said, tugging at Matt's arm. "Let go!"

Matt kept hold of the branch. "We . . . we can't just drop him."

"We leave him here. We run to tell someone!"

"What if he drowns?"

Rachel stared at Matt. "You do not know who he is."

"Of course I know! He dropped bombs all over Canterbury, and—"

"He fights for murderers. For Nazis. To help them murder."

"Yeah, but . . . but he's just air crew. I mean, I hope they put him jail and throw away the key, but he's only a soldier."

"I am just a soldier," the pilot called, his voice softer. "You are right. I should not have lied."

"Why did you?"

"I am scared! I bailed out in the enemy territory. For me, this is the scariest moment of my life."

"Let's go, Matt!" Rachel urged.

Matt rubbed his face. What would Eric do? He couldn't tell. "I—I don't know . . ."

"I'm only a regular bloke," the pilot said. "I was drafted into the Luftwaffe. The German air force. I always loved airplanes, since I was your age."

"I . . ." Matt swallowed. "I like airplanes too."

"They trained me. They sent me on my very first bombing run . . . and I am shot from the sky. And worse, about to drown in a little stream."

"We can't let him drown." Matt tied the parachute cords around the branch to keep it in place.

"We need to get him out of there."

Rachel didn't say anything. She didn't even tug on her braid.

"Then we'll turn him in," Matt said. "But first we need to save his life."

Rachel just looked at him with her dark eyes.

"Fine," Matt said. "I'll do it myself."

He approached the water, and for once Rachel didn't follow him. Reeling in the parachute cord had brought the pilot—well, the *German*—to the very edge of the canal. If the man hadn't been wrapped in cord, he could've just pulled himself onto firm ground.

But the cords twined tightly around him. He was trapped.

He looked up at Matt with pleading eyes. "I give you my word. I will surrender myself to a soldier."

The German smelled of canal water and machine oil when Matt knelt beside him. "Okay."

"Pull me up."

Matt yanked and tugged. He grabbed a handful of the German's flight suit and heaved until finally the German squirmed onto the ground.

"Ah!" the German said. "Thank you."

"Yeah, um . . ." Matt didn't know what to say. "Is your head okay?"

"Only a scratch." With shaking hands, the German unstrapped his parachute harness. "Ah. Much better."

"So I guess we should find someone . . ."

"What are the chances, eh? To fly across the Channel and land here?" The German looked around. "A pretty city, Canterbury."

"Yeah, I guess."

The German removed his helmet. "And this is a quiet little corner."

"It's, um, a park."

"I count myself lucky that I did not fall into the downtown."

"Yeah, it's on fire." Matt didn't say, "Because you were dropping bombs on it."

"And here we are. Nobody knows I am here, except my two . . . how do you say? Someone who rescues a person."

"Um, a rescuer?"

"A savior! My two saviors." The German looked around. "If I hide my chute and change my clothes? Well, then, perhaps nobody will capture me. Perhaps I'll stay free."

A dagger of fear stabbed Matt's heart. "Except you gave your word about turning yourself in."

"Of course!" The German raised his hands as if he were surrendering. "Of course, I am just thinking out loud."

"So I guess we should—"

"One question," the German interrupted. "Do you know if there is an English saying about how much a promise is worth in wartime?"

The fear throbbed in Matt's chest. "Um, no."

"Well, boy . . ." When the German shifted, a combat knife gleamed in his right hand. "It is not worth much."

"You promised—"

The German grabbed Matt's arm and raised the blade. "I cannot let you tell anyone that I am here."

"Rachel!" Matt yelled, trying to break free. "Run!"

CHAPTER 20

"**H**ere!" Landry's packmate shouted. "Bring the dog here!"

"C'mon, Chief," Landry said. "Here, boy."

Chief ignored him for a moment, standing atop a heap of overturned earth and charred wood. He'd caught Matt's scent again, somewhere in the distance, along with a whiff of grass and river water. . . .

Then the wind shifted, and all Chief smelled were bitter fumes and the guts of fallen buildings.

"Chief!" Landry shouted again. "Come!"

Chief darted down into the road. The man needed him. He flashed around a cluster of firemen and stopped beside Landry. He didn't hear any special threat. He smelled blistering metal and charred plastic, but he didn't sense any looming danger.

"Over here," the first man said, standing outside a brick building. "I heard something inside this movie theater."

Landry jogged to the man. "Where exactly?"

"I don't know," the man said. "I can't hear it anymore."

"C'mere, boy," Landry said, calling Chief into the building. "Find. *Find*, Chief."

Chief trotted into the ruins of a big den with rows of chairs and a high ceiling with holes blasted through it. The air smelled of cigarette smoke even more than fire smoke. The creak and clatter of settling debris sounded faintly from the far corner.

"A high-explosive bomb hit," the man told Landry. "I thought I heard something while we were clearing the building."

Landry looked at Chief.

Chief looked at Landry.

"Well," Landry told the man. "You didn't."

"How do you know? Make him check!"

"He already checked," Landry said. "He checked before he set foot inside."

"Are you sure?"

"Have you ever heard of a dog named Jet?" Landry asked, heading outside. "He's a German shepherd like Chief here. With maybe a little collie in him too."

Chief looked up at the sound of his name. Landry didn't seem to need any help, though, so he paused on the sidewalk to listen to the rest of the street.

"Jet's an English dog," Landry told the man. "They say he rescued a hundred people during the Blitz, when the Germans bombed London."

"A hundred people! You're pulling my leg."

"Maybe even more. Before that, he worked for a year guarding airfields, but search and rescue is in his blood. Most dogs—most animals, well, most *everyone*—is scared of fire. But Jet? He'd run into burning buildings to save people. He'd run through the fire."

"Like your dog did," the man say.

"He's not my dog," Landry said, resting a hand on Chief's ruff. "But that's right. That's how I knew he was special. Jet's handler has to hold him back to keep him from running into the flames to save people."

"Whoa, that's some kind of brave."

"Yeah. Jet once raced into a factory full of poison smoke. His nose is so good he found the one survivor in the entire place."

"You think Chief's like that?"

"Like I told you," Landry said. "He's a natural. He's—"

"Running off," the man said, from behind Chief as he loped toward a sudden gust of the metallic smell of blood.

Why did humans spend so much time yipping to each other? Couldn't they hear the far-off whistles through the smoke? Couldn't they smell the human fear-scent wafting from down the block?

Chief scrambled over a pile of rubble. A sharp metal edge ripped out a hunk of his fur but didn't cut his skin. He barked for Landry and the other man to hurry.

"I'm coming!" Landry yelled. "I've only got two legs."

Chief rounded a corner and found two women helping an injured man. He trotted closer and sniffed the air. He smelled more injured people. The women already knew about them, though. He could tell because of the scent trails.

"Hello?" Landry called to the women. "US Army here! Do you need help?"

"Not as much as they do," one woman said, pointing to the injured people.

"Oh!" Landry looked from the wounded people back to the women. "You're ATS. I thought you stayed in shelters during raids."

"You're Americans," the woman said. "I thought you stayed in cowboy hats."

Landry laughed and helped the women tend the wounded people. Chief watched approvingly for a moment, then cocked his head as a far-off whistle sounded sharper and closer.

Chief started to bark a warning, then caught the faintest whiff of Rachel. Where was she? He inhaled deeply. He smelled Matt, too, and a musky dampness. Not too far—

The whistling grew louder, dragging his attention back to his surroundings. A shrill, deadly sound. Falling directly toward this street.

Fire-rocks were going to hit Landry and the women!

CHAPTER 21

Matt tried to pull away, but the German's grip was too tight. The man's eyes narrowed. Blood oozed down his cheek, and water dripped from his flight suit.

"W-we saved your life!" Matt said.

"For which I thank you." The German raised his voice. "Girl! Show yourself! Come here, or your brother will be sorry!"

Matt tried to kick the German but missed. "Run, Rachel!"

"Enough!" The German shook him roughly.

"I don't have time to waste on—"

Thunk.

The German blinked at Matt.

He released his grip and swayed.

Matt ripped free from the man's loosening grip and saw Rachel standing behind him. Holding the thick branch like a baseball bat. Just like Matt had taught her.

She'd clubbed him in the head.

When Rachel pulled back for another swing, the German spun toward her! He swore and knocked the branch from her hands.

Matt tried to kick him again—and this time he succeeded.

The German, still tangled in the cords, stumbled a few steps.

"Run!" Matt shouted to Rachel. "C'mon, c'mon, *c'mon!*"

He dashed past the German, grabbed Rachel's wrist, and raced into the darkness.

A tree loomed.

Bushes tugged at his pajama legs.

Footsteps sounded behind them. A sort of shuffling drag as the German limped. But still moving fast. Too fast.

The German was gaining on them!

A wall loomed in front of Matt. He yanked Rachel to one side and lunged through a doorway into an alley.

He couldn't tell which way to go. He was too scared to focus, too scared to think.

He ran blindly ahead. Were they on Beer Cart Lane? St. Margaret's Street? He didn't know, he couldn't tell.

Sirens and shouts filled the air. Engines and explosions and smoke. More bombs were dropping! More bombs than ever.

Another wave of German bombers flew overhead, dropping hundreds of incendiary and high-explosive bombs. Yet the loudest things were Matt's pounding heartbeat . . . and the scuff of footsteps behind them.

He and Rachel sped around a corner, they raced across a street. Matt pulled Rachel into the thicker shadows of a building and risked a peek over his shoulder.

He didn't see the German. The streets looked deserted and—

Shuffle-drag, shuffle-drag.

There!

The German prowled forward. His knife gleamed in the reflected light of a fire.

"We need to find soldiers!" Matt pulled Rachel faster down the street. "Or firemen."

"Then we should run *toward* the flames." Rachel's braid flapped wildly around her shoulders. "That is where they'll be."

"That's the worst idea I've ever heard!"

"So what should we do?"

"Run toward the flames!" Matt said, stumbling into an intersection. "Like you said!"

The terrifying whistle of falling bombs sounded all around and above them. Every street looked like a minefield. If they took one wrong turn . . .

"It's another wave of bombing," Matt said. "The biggest one yet!"

"Where is the fire?" Rachel asked, blinking at the rooftops.

After taking a nervous glance behind them, Matt peered into the smoky sky.

An orange glow gleamed on the thick smoke

suffocating Canterbury. But where was the glow brightest? Matt couldn't tell. He looked for the cathedral steeple, but he couldn't even see the roofs of the buildings surrounding them. He hoped his parents were still in the shelter, still safe, and that Chief was—

Shuffle-drag, shuffle-drag. The sound of the German's limping footsteps came from a cloud of dust and smoke billowing down a nearby street.

Matt's breath caught—and the rhythm changed. *Shuffle-shuffle, shuffle-shuffle.* The German had spotted them! He was closing in!

Terror pricked at Matt's skin. "This way!" he gasped, fleeing across the intersection with Rachel.

An ambulance pulled into view down the block. A dingy pool of light spilled from the hooded headlights.

"Help!" Matt screamed.

"Over here!" Rachel yelled.

His mind reeling in fear, Matt raced forward, shouting and waving, but the driver didn't see or hear him. The ambulance turned the corner and vanished into the smoke.

Matt and Rachel ran after the ambulance, trying to catch it, but they couldn't keep up. Weaving around the rubble covering the street, they raced for safety—away from the German.

Matt listened for the shuffling limp, but he heard a shrill whistle instead.

There was a clatter on the rooftops.

A scraping sound, then a *clunk*.

An incendiary firebomb had fallen nearby!

CHAPTER 22

"The bomb is in front of us!" Rachel said. "There, on the sidewalk!"

"Where? Are you sure?"

"It's right there, Matt!"

"We can't turn around! Jerry's behind us and—"

"It's *right there*!"

Rachel shoved Matt backward. He almost fell, then caught his balance. He didn't see the bomb, so he couldn't tell which way to run!

Through his panic-stricken eyes, the street

seemed to turn into a maze of fire and death—and he froze.

Then Rachel tugged Matt's hand, and he unfroze. He felt a flash of relief as he followed her. He didn't always *need* to know what to do. Sometimes he could rely on his friends.

As they raced back along the smoke-filled street, a flare of light burned suddenly behind them when the firebomb ignited. Heat smacked the back of Matt's neck.

He ran until the heat faded, then glanced at Rachel. "I guess it was right there."

"Are you *sure*?" she asked.

He snorted. "Where is he? We need to—"

Shuffle-drag, shuffle-drag! From the smoke and darkness in front of them, the German trotted closer.

"Listen!" Rachel said.

"I hear him! He's coming—"

"Not him," she said. "Voices!"

Then Matt heard them too. Men calling to each other in the next street, men with English accents. Civil defense workers or firemen. Men who would save them!

if you do anything to us, they'll know you're here."

"You are just two foolish young children," the man said. "Caught in an air raid. Nobody will look twice."

"Help!" Rachel screamed.

"There is no help," the man said, limping forward.

The orange glow of fire touched the smoke above the city, but the alley itself was as dark as a nightmare. Matt felt tears in his eyes. He wanted to cry. For himself, for Rachel. For Eric. For his parents.

He swallowed instead. He put one arm protectively in front of Rachel and backed closer to the end of the alley.

The dead end.

A brick wall rose behind them, two stories high.

"Help!" Rachel yelled again.

"It is time to be quiet," the German said, stalking closer. "As quiet as the grave."

"Chief!" Matt shouted. *"Chief!"*

CHAPTER 23

Chief's ears pricked, tracking the whistling sound through the air. One of the fire-rocks would land right where Landry and the women were standing!

And somehow they didn't know. They couldn't hear. *Humans!*

Chief sprang forward and barked at them.

"Goodness!" one of the women said. "What does he want?"

"He hears someone in the buildings," Landry

said. "Chief, find!"

Chief barked again. *Move, move!*

"What is it, boy?" Landry asked.

"Is he part wolf?" the other woman said. "He's a trifle . . . fierce."

"Don't worry," Landry said. "He won't hurt you or—"

The whistling grew louder. Closer. Chief raised his ruff and started growling, deep in his throat.

"Er," Landry said. "I think."

Chief laid his ears flat against his head and growled at the women. A fire-rock hit on the other side of the buildings. Then another one, closer. But the humans still didn't notice.

Chief growled louder and slunk at the woman, low and sleek.

Still holding the man on the stretcher, the women backed quickly away from his bared teeth. They weren't stupid.

Landry crouched down. "What's *wrong*, boy?"

The shrill whistles of the fire-rocks were speeding at them. This wasn't the time for yipping! This was the time for action.

So Chief leaped at Landry and knocked him to the ground.

"Hey!" Landry shouted, rolling away. "Bad dog!"

Chief nipped his leg and nipped his arm.

Landry kept rolling, and the women with the injured man kept backing away. Chief raised his gaze from Landry and bared his teeth at them until they moved behind the car.

"What is he doing?" the woman said. "What's wrong with him?"

When Chief growled at her, Landry shoved him away and tried to stand. He steadied himself—

And Chief jumped on top of him, as hard as he could.

Landry fell with an "Oof!"

"He's attacking!" one of the women yelled. "He's run mad! Watch out, he—"

The fire-rock slammed into the ground where they'd been standing moments before. The blast exploded into Chief's side and flung him off Landry.

His ears rang painfully, and his vision blurred.

The smell of brick dust assaulted his nostrils—
and he thought he heard Matt's voice calling,
"Chief, help!"

The sky swirled above Chief, and he couldn't
tell what he'd heard over the throbbing in his ears.

The scents dulled, and the buildings seemed
to wobble.

"He—he saved you," one of the women said,
after the dust had settled.

"He saved us all," the other woman said.

Landry knelt beside Chief and touched his
side gently. "Chief? Chief. I've got you. I've got
you. *Shh*. What a good boy. What a good, *good*
boy."

Chief licked his hand.

"I'll never doubt you again, boy," Landry said.
"Not ever."

"How bad is it?" one of the women asked.

Landry's fingers touched Chief's coat here
and there, as soft as butterflies. "I think he's okay.
Thank God. He got the wind knocked out of
him, that's all."

The world still wobbled around Chief, though.
And had he really heard Matt calling for him? He

thought he'd heard Rachel too. Except he must've imagined the two pups yelling for him, because now everything sounded muffled and far away.

Chief tried to stand. His legs were too weak. Landry held him tight and said his name, over and over.

Chief smelled the relief on Landry. He smelled affection. He listened closer, but he couldn't hear Matt or Rachel. He couldn't hear anything.

CHAPTER 24

The German stalked closer, his knife swaying like a snake.

Matt backed to the end of the alley, keeping Rachel behind him until she hit the wall. A dark niche opened to Matt's right, and a pile of shattered bricks stood to his left. A bomb must've smashed one of the surrounding buildings.

There was nowhere to run.

The German pointed his blade at Rachel, and fear almost stopped Matt's heart.

His knees wobbled, and his throat clenched.

Still, he knew what Eric would do if he were here. He knew what Eric would do if someone threatened *Matt* with a knife.

With a fearful whimper, Matt stepped toward the German—and shoved Rachel into the dark niche beside them.

He was trying to protect her, trying to keep her away from the German.

Except instead of hitting the wall and stopping, she kept going. She tripped over a plank on the floor and yelped.

Not a plank, a *door*. A door that had been ripped from its hinges by the bombing and thrown to the ground.

Rachel stumbled through the open doorway and vanished inside the big square building.

She yelled Matt's name.

The German cursed and lunged.

But in a flash, Matt followed Rachel.

He shot across the wobbling door. He lost his balance and sprawled to the rubble-filled floor of the building—but he didn't stop moving.

He crawled frantically forward, down a long corridor that led deeper into the space. Rachel appeared from the gloomy darkness and helped him to stand.

The German lost his balance on the shattered door behind them. He swore as he fell with a crash. He was bigger and heavier than a kid; he thrashed and struggled instead of just hopping back onto his feet.

Matt and Rachel ran farther into the dark corridor. Matt's mouth tasted of dust and ash. His pajama shirt was damp and speckled with burn marks from embers.

Rachel pulled him past a pile of crates and two closed doors. Then the corridor ended in a pile of debris.

A wall of wood and concrete must have blasted through from the next room. The dullest glimmering of light brushed shattered glass and scorched cloth.

"Can we climb over?" Matt asked.

Rachel peered into the darkness. "I do not think so."

"Quick." Matt spun around, turning toward the German. He groped in the pitch-dark for Rachel's hand, then led her back the way they'd come. "Hurry!"

He tried the first door. It was locked.

The German coughed nearby, invisible in the gloom. His boots scuffed through the debris on the floor. Ten feet away. Five.

Matt froze, holding Rachel's hand.

Neither of them spoke. Neither of them breathed.

The limping scuffle sounded closer.

Closer.

Then the German stopped. Just two feet from them. Matt could smell cigarettes and canal water.

The *shuffle-drag* moved past them, heading for the pile of debris filling the corridor.

Moving mouse-quiet, Matt crept closer to the opening to the alley. Once they got back to the street, they could run for help!

He tiptoed one step.

Then another.

Then his foot landed on a loose bit of concrete

or twisted metal. The scrape sounded loud in the dark corridor.

"Ha!" the German said, from the darkness. "I thought I—"

Matt lunged for the knob of the second door. He turned it desperately and flung the door open!

He burst through, pulling Rachel along with him, and slammed the door behind them.

When he turned, he found himself inside a movie theater.

Rows of chairs faced the stage . . . except for the ones torn and toppled by a blast. A balcony rose along one wall. The faint white rectangle of the screen seemed to hover in the darkness. A wide gash opened in the ceiling high above, and the orange glow of fire raging outside seeped through, giving a tinge of light.

Not enough to keep Matt from slamming his shin twice before finding the aisle between the chairs.

"Crawl!" he whispered to Rachel, falling to his hands and knees.

The door slammed open behind them. The German stepped inside.

Shuffle-drag.

Shuffle-drag.

Matt and Rachel crawled between the chairs. Across the wreckage-covered floor toward the wall. Under the balcony, the movie theater seemed to darken.

Shuffle-drag, shuffle-drag.

Matt's breathing sounded loud and harsh. He crawled behind Rachel until she reached the wall.

Rachel put her hand on his arm and whispered. "There is no way out. Just wall."

The *shuffle-drag* sounded closer, and Matt prayed that the German couldn't see them. But when he peered into the half-ruined movie theater, the first thing he saw was the glint of the German's eyes.

Looking directly at him.

"You ran the good race," the German said, prowling between the chairs to stand over Matt. "But now you have reached the finish."

CHAPTER 25

Matt scooted backward against Rachel, trying to get away from the German.

He retreated until he couldn't move any farther. He felt Rachel's breath on the back of his neck. He saw the German standing above him, silhouetted by the dim light that seeped through the hole in the ceiling.

The German drew back his knife. Matt raised his arm—

A *SMASH-clatter-clatter* sounded in the balcony above them.

"Huh," the German grunted.

Matt peeked between his arms, and a noise tore through the theater. So loud that it that felt like a thousand firecrackers going off. Too loud for an incendiary firebomb. It was a high-explosive bomb detonating on the roof above them!

The blast blew through the ceiling and smashed balcony chairs into splinters. A rain of wood chunks pelted the theater. Bits of wood and plaster fell around Matt and Rachel and bounced off the German's shoulders.

Rachel clung to Matt, and he gripped her arms tightly in a terrified daze. He couldn't think. He couldn't move . . . and a terrible *crack* sounded overhead.

The edge of the balcony swung down toward them.

The German dodged, barely avoiding getting smashed. He dove away from Matt and Rachel, racing for the exit, while Matt gaped in shock.

The balcony stopped falling five feet over-head. It hung from a dozen half-shattered planks directly above Matt and Rachel. Dust swirled in the dim orange light, bent metal struts groaned.

And then, with the snapping of wood and the moan of railings, the balcony started to collapse completely.

"Rachel!" Matt yelled, shoving her away from the danger zone.

She scrambled away—

And a chunk of balcony slammed down.

Pain flared in Matt's legs, and dust clogged his nose. At first he saw nothing but blackness. He heard nothing except the crash, still echoing in his mind. Yet as the dust cloud from the bomb settled, his vision cleared. With another section of the ceiling blasted away, more orange light seeped into the room.

From behind him, Matt heard Rachel crying and calling his name.

"He's gone!" he said, without looking at her. "I think he's gone."

His leg ached as he shifted—and he found himself staring at the remaining section of the broken balcony, dangling above him. If that one fell, they'd be in trouble. Well, in even more trouble.

Matt swallowed a mouthful of dust and ash

and peered quickly across the theater. The German was gone. Either he figured that Matt and Rachel were dead in the crash, or he was afraid the building was going to fall on him.

Which made sense. The whole place could collapse at any moment.

Matt pushed himself onto his knees.

Creak!

The section of balcony above him swayed and creaked. He needed to run! He needed to escape!

He reached for Rachel . . . but she wasn't there.

Instead, the fallen bit of balcony covered the corner of the theater between him and the wall.

"Rachel?" he yelled, frantic with fear. "Rachel, say something! Are you there? Can you hear—"

A little voice came from beneath the collapsed balcony. "Matt!"

Matt almost fainted in relief. "Are you okay?"

"Stuck . . . ," Rachel said.

Matt rolled to his side. Pain throbbed in his leg, but he reached along the fallen balcony until he found a small opening. "Rachel?"

The darkness shifted beneath the rubble. "Matt?"

"I'm right here." He poked his arm into the opening. "I'm here."

A soft hand curled around his wrist. "Are you hurt?"

"I'm fine," he said, not looking at his leg. "How about you?"

"Not even a scratch," she said, her voice trembling. "Except I'm stuck. I can't get out."

He looked at the rubble separating them. There was way too much for him to move. Plus, what if he tried to dig Rachel out and everything collapsed on her?

"Don't worry," he said, trying not to let his fear sound in his voice. "We'll find a way."

She didn't speak for a moment. Then she tried to make a joke. "You finally get your wish. If you leave, I can't tag along with you."

"I'm not going anywhere. You were right all along. We need to stick together."

A sniffle came from the darkness.

"You're the bravest kid I know," Matt said. "Boy howdy! You socked a Nazi with a stick!"

"Like Eric," she said.

"Just like Eric," Matt said, feeling tears prick

his eyes. "You and me, we're a team."

"Yes but . . . you must run before the roof falls."

"I'm not leaving without you. You're my sister. We stick together."

Rachel squeezed his hand. After a minute, she said, "I know I will never see them again. My mother and father. My sisters. My family."

"Maybe you—"

"I will never see them again, Matt," she said, and the tone in her voice silenced him completely.

Another silence fell, and this time he squeezed her hand.

"I will never see them again," she repeated, "and I cannot lose another family. You have to go. Run for help."

"I won't leave you."

"Come back with help!" she said. "Find help and come back."

"I'm not leaving you, Rachel. I don't care what—"

Creak.

Crash!

The noise burst from above Matt. When he looked upward, the final section of balcony seemed to fall at him in slow motion.

Pipes skewed into the air. Sparks flew, and wooden beams tore.

And with a *slam* the balcony crashed down around Matt. It didn't hit him, but it surrounded him. The dim orange light turned pitch-black.

Matt groped with his hands and his injured legs, and he couldn't feel a way out.

Now he was trapped too.

CHAPTER 26

Even after Chief shook the ringing from his ears, the car's engine sounded dull as the women drove away. The whistle of fire-rocks still shrilled, but not too close.

The scent of fresh blood felt like a sharp tang in Chief's nose. He sniffed the area where the injured people had been. No, that's not what he was smelling.

He turned his head to Landry, who knelt beside him.

"Good boy," Landry was still saying. "You're a real champ."

Chief nudged the human's shoulder, which was damp with blood.

"Ow! Oh!" Landry tugged at his shirt. "When did that happen?"

Chief tried to knock away Landry's hand, to give the wound a few healthful licks. Landry didn't let him, though. That was fine. Chief didn't insist. Sometimes you needed to lick your own wounds.

Landry probed his shoulder. "It's just a scratch. Still, you should've told me a few minutes ago. That pretty ATS girl could've bandaged me."

The wound smelled okay, so Chief turned and loped back toward the area with the ruined buildings. That's where people needed help. And it's also the direction from which he thought he'd heard the girl-pup and boy-pup.

"Okay, okay," Landry said, trotting beside him. "Slow down, four legs."

When they reached the street, Chief sniffed for people inside the buildings. He pricked his ears to listen, too, but the world still sounded far away. As he cocked his head, the up-and-down machine yowling changed into a loud howl.

"It's the all-clear siren!" another man told Landry. "Hey—you're bleeding."

"I caught a splinter."

"Sit down. Let's get you patched up."

"I can't, I've got to patrol with Chief. The raid's over, but his work is just starting."

"Patrol after you're bandaged, soldier!" the man said. "That's not a request. Give the dog to one of your buddies."

So Landry tied a rope to Chief's collar and handed the other end to another man. Chief eyed the man dubiously. He probably wasn't as well trained as Landry. Still, as long as he knew how to follow a leash, he'd be okay.

While another human started wrapping Landry's wound, Chief led his new man along the street. The smoke grew thicker even though the iron birds were gone.

And a hint of sweat and fear wafted from beneath a pile of rubble.

CHAPTER 27

Bombs fell outside. Sirens screamed.

Matt curled onto his side and hugged his knees. He'd lost Eric. He'd lost Chief. He'd lost his parents, and he hadn't even kept Rachel safe. Instead, he'd gotten her trapped in a bombed-out building.

He blinked back tears as he listened to Rachel cry. Maybe he cried too.

Finally the noise quieted. Both the tears and the bombs.

"Do you think the raid is over?" Rachel said

into the darkness.

"Either that or there are more waves coming."

"There can't be! When will it stop? When will— Oh!"

"What?"

"I heard people!" Rachel took a breath. "Help! Help!"

"We're in the movie theater!" Matt yelled, even though he didn't hear anyone. "We're trapped!"

"Help! Anyone!"

They yelled and yelled, but nobody answered. Nobody heard.

"It's no good," Matt said, his throat aching. "The balcony's padded. It's muffling our voices."

"'Muffling' isn't a word," Rachel said.

"It is too."

"English is silly," she said. "Muffling."

Matt smiled in the darkness. "It's softening our voices."

"Maybe we should . . . Do you remember what Eric taught us? About Morse code?"

"Brilliant!" Matt said. "We can tap out an SOS!"

"That's the signal for help?"

"Yeah," Matt said. "It goes 'dot-dot-dot, dash-dash-dash, dot-dot-dot.'"

"I remember now!"

"Do you have anything to tap with?" Matt reached in the darkness, wincing at a twinge of pain in his knee. "There's a pipe here. And a . . . I think it's a chair leg or something."

"I have a piece of lamp." Rachel made a long scraping noise on the other side of the balcony. "Like that."

Matt tapped the chair leg against the pipe. *Clunk, clunk, clunk. Clunk, clunk, clunk. Clunk, clunk, clunk.* "That sounds like dot-dot-dot, dot-dot-dot, dot-dot-dot."

"Start over again."

Matt tapped the chair leg. *Clunk, clunk, clunk. Cl—*

Scraaape, came from Rachel's section under the balcony. *Scraaape. Scraaape.*

Clunk, clunk, clunk, Matt tapped. *Clunk, clunk, clunk.*

Scraaape. Scraaape. Scraaape.

Clunk, clunk, clunk.

"Maybe the balcony is moffling this too," Rachel said.

"Muffling," Matt corrected.

Rachel giggled. "I am teasing!"

"We're trapped in a bombed building, and you're making jokes?"

"Only a very bad joke," she said. *Scraaape. Scraaape. Scraaape.*

"That's okay then." Matt smiled in the darkness and tapped the pipe. "I hope my folks are okay."

"And Chief."

"I'm sure he's fine. He's tough. He's Eric's dog. Nothing bad can . . ." Matt trailed off when he remembered that Eric was MIA. "Can happen to him."

Neither of them spoke while he tapped and Rachel scraped out SOS-SOS-SOS.

"You should not have yelled at your parents," Rachel eventually said. "Back in the shelter. You should not have yelled."

"They shouldn't have let Eric join the army

so early! They should've kept him with us. With the family. At home. We need him." Matt's tears came more easily this time. "I . . . miss him. All the time."

"If I had my parents, I would never yell at them."

"If you had a brother, you would." *Clunk, clunk, clunk.* "You'd yell at your parents if they let him leave and he went missing."

She didn't say anything. She just went *scraaape, scraaape, scraaape,* and Matt realized that she'd give anything just to have parents to yell at.

"Anyway, you *do* have a brother," Matt said. "Me."

She stopped scraping. Matt heard her move on the other side of the fallen balcony, like she'd turned to look at him.

"What would you do if *I* went MIA?" he asked her.

"I would yell," Rachel said.

"Good," he said.

"Except not— Oh! Oh, do you hear?"

Matt cocked his head in the darkness and

heard a single long blare of the sirens. "That's the all-clear sign! The raid's over!"

"There are people nearby too," she said.

Sure enough, faint shouts sounded from the street outside the theater.

"There's nobody in there," a man's voice said.

"The movie theater's clear?" another voice said.

"Hello?" Matt called. "Hello?"

"We're trapped!" Rachel shouted in her accented voice. "Help!"

The men didn't hear them.

"We already checked in there," the first man said. "Move out."

"We're in here!" Matt shouted at the top of his lungs.

The voices faded away . . . then Matt heard a distant bark.

"Is that Chief?" Rachel asked.

"Chief!" Matt shouted. "Chief! We're in here!"

Two sharp barks.

"Chief!" Rachel yelled. "Chief!"

"What is that mutt doing?" a voice said. "We've got a situation around the corner. Get a wiggle on!"

Matt and Rachel screamed and shouted, but the men's voices grew fainter and fainter.

Until they all disappeared—even Chief's.

And Matt and Rachel were alone again.

CHAPTER 28

3 A.M.

Chief dragged the man toward the ruined building. The man was so slow! And clumsy. He kept pulling in the wrong direction.

Chief gripped the ground with his claws and tugged until he pulled the man toward the building. Toward Matt.

A few other men were walking past. "We've already checked the movie theater. Search somewhere else."

Matt's voice sounded faintly from inside the building—and a whisper of Rachel's voice.

The humans didn't hear, so he barked louder.

"This way, Chief!" the man said.

Chief lunged toward the doors of the building.

"What is that mutt doing?" another man said. "We've got a situation around the corner. Move him along!"

Chief barked and barked.

"Silly dog just wants to watch a movie," the man said.

Together the two men started dragging Chief away from the building. Chief hunkered down and pulled, but he couldn't budge two men at once. Not without biting them, and Eric had taught him not to bite.

"Hey!" Landry ran toward Chief with his unfinished bandage flapping. "Can't you hear him?"

"He's trying to get into the theater," the other men said. "There's nobody there."

"There is if Chief thinks so," Landry said.

"The dog cleared it himself earlier. You believe someone ran *into* a bombed building?"

Landry looked at Chief. He looked at the men. Then he untied the leash and said, "I believe

whatever this dog tells me."

Chief raced toward the building with Landry stumbling along behind him. A pile of debris filled the front door. Chief paced. How could they get inside?

"Around back," Landry said.

"Private Landry!" another man yelled. "Stand down! We need that dog around the cor—"

"Someone needs our help right here!"

"Can *you* hear them? We don't take orders from a mutt."

"No, I—" Landry quieted.

Clunk, clunk, clunk.

Scraaape. Scraaape. Scraaape.

Clunk, clunk, clunk.

"Yes. Yes, I can."

"That's an SOS," the other man said. "The fleabag is right! Someone's buried in the rubble!"

CHAPTER 29

When Matt heard Chief barking again, he wiped the tears from his eyes. "He's coming back."

"Chief?" Rachel asked.

"I knew he'd come back. I knew it."

Still, Matt tapped louder for a few minutes, and Rachel scraped harder as the sound of rummaging through rubble came from outside.

"Hello?" a man called.

"Hi! Hello!" Matt and Rachel yelled. "We're in here!"

Chief barked.

"Chief!" Matt shouted.

Three more barks sounded, sharper and louder.

"Good boy!" Matt yelled.

"Good bear!" Rachel yelled.

Matt sensed that the man was squatting down next to the rubble. "You know Chief?"

"He's my brother's dog!" Matt said.

"He's really something," the man called, as the sound of rummaging continued outside. "He heard your SOS. That's pretty spiffy, a dog who understands Morse code."

That was a really stupid joke, almost as bad as Rachel's. Still, Matt smiled—mostly from relief.

"What're your names?" the man asked.

"I'm Matt," Matt said. "My sister is Rachel."

Chief barked.

"I'm Landry. Private Landry of the US Army. We'll have you out of there in a few minutes." His voice seemed to deepen. "Is anyone else in there? Anyone hurt?"

"No," Matt said. "We're okay."

"Matt's hurt," Rachel said.

Matt wrinkled his nose. How did Rachel know about that? "My leg's a little banged up is all. Um, are you American?"

"I am!" Private Landry said.

"So'm I! What're you doing here?"

"I could ask you the same question! You chose a bad time to catch the double feature."

A scrape and clatter sounded as rescuers shifted the rubble, trying to get to Matt and Rachel. The noise sent a shiver of fear into Matt's heart, and he heard Rachel gasp.

"What's happening?" Matt asked.

"This is going to take a few minutes," Private Landry said. "Don't worry, I'm not going anywhere. I've got a scratch, and now I'm stuck here getting bandaged."

"Good," Rachel said, her voice a little shaky. "You stay here."

"It would've been worse than a scratch if not for Chief," Private Landry said. "He saved me. He's a whiz of a rescue dog."

"Rescue dog?"

"He's a natural," Private Landry said, and

launched into a story about Chief's adventures that night.

Matt figured that the American soldier was just talking to keep him and Rachel calm, but he didn't mind. He liked it, actually. And it really was keeping him and Rachel calm, despite the throbbing pain in his leg and the grinding of the rubble being cleared.

"Have you heard of Dogs for Defense?" Private Landry asked.

Matt shook his head in the darkness. "I don't think so."

"It started earlier this year. Dog breeders and trainers joined together to train guard dogs for the War Department."

A metallic groan sounded, and the balcony trembled two feet above Matt's head. He almost yelped—he almost burst into tears—but he needed to stay strong for Rachel. So he only whimpered and said a silent prayer.

"The army doesn't even have a place to keep all those dogs," Private Landry continued, "forget about training them. So dozens of private kennels around the country are volunteering to house and train them. That's how I heard. My aunt owns a kennel."

"You are a trainer of dogs?" Rachel asked.

"My aunt is," Landry said, and the balcony shifted again. "Most of the army dogs are donated from private families, but the training program is moving pretty slowly so far. That's why Chief is so remarkable."

"Because he's so quick?" Matt asked, trying to keep his voice steady as he eyed the balcony.

"Yeah. He reminds me of a dog I heard about on the front lines. This dog's platoon got cut off from base. They were out there all alone, under heavy fire, with no way to ask for help against the Germans."

"Against Nazis," Rachel said.

Landry gave a little laugh. "That's right. So the soldiers attached a phone cable to the dog's collar, and he ran through enemy territory, dodging gunfire and shells until he reached the base. The platoon used the cable to call for backup, and they survived, all on account of that dog."

"That's amazing!" Matt said.

"Yeah. Like Chief here."

Chief barked.

"That's right, boy," Landry said, before raising his voice again. "He doesn't run from fire or fumes. He doesn't run from *bombs*. He knows if someone's trapped, and he'll fight for them. He's some kind of hero, this dog. All he cares about is saving lives."

"My brother . . ." Matt took a breath. "My brother, Eric, trained him."

"Then he's a hero too. Chief is the kind of dog the army needs. He's a real soldier dog. If he—"

Chief barked again, more urgently. Was he warning them? Was the building about to collapse?

"Hey, wat—" Matt started to shout at them to be careful—and all in a rush, a pile of rubble shifted. "Chief, no!"

CHAPTER 30

Matt's stomach dropped. His breath caught. Was the building falling on him and Rachel even as rescuers tried to dig them free?

Then a gap formed in the rubble. Faint light gleamed from outside, and cool smoky air billowed around Matt. The rescuers had done it! They'd dug a way out!

"C'mon, kid," a man's gruff voice said. "Movie's over."

"Where's Rachel?" Matt asked. "You need to help Ra—"

"I'm right here!" Rachel said from in front of him. She'd been trapped against the building's wall, so they'd reached her first.

"Oh!" Matt exhaled in relief.

Matt crawled toward the light, following Rachel's feet. Pain throbbed in his leg, and rubble scraped him through his pajamas.

A pair of strong hands lifted Rachel from the rubble, and then the gruff voice murmured to her, "You're safe, lass. We've got you now."

Matt squirmed forward, and another man hefted Matt from the rubble. This one had a bandaged shoulder and a warm smile. A rope-leash looped around his wrist and dangled on the floor. "I'm Bert Landry."

"Matt," Matt said. "Matt Dawson."

The gruff man asked Matt, "So is Chief your dog?"

"Or are you Chief's boy?" Landry asked, bringing Matt to the wreckage-strewn street.

Matt smiled. "A little bit of both, I guess."

"Well, he's—"

Two paws landed on Matt's chest, and a wet tongue licked his face. "Chief!" he cried. "I was so

worried about you!"

Chief licked Matt twice more. Then Matt got a face full of wagging tail as Chief turned to lick Rachel.

"Chiefy!" Rachel said, and fell to her knees to give Chief a hug.

Matt coughed from the smoke and dust as he looked at the people who'd rescued them. A couple of American GIs stood nearby, and Matt recognized a familiar sedan: the ATS women were there too. And British firemen and air-raid wardens and civil defense workers were scattered in the street beyond them.

The destroyed street.

Through the thick smoke still pouring from blazing fires, Matt saw that half of the buildings had been completely flattened. The sight made him a little faint, and he grabbed hold of Landry's arm to keep from falling.

"I know, kid," Landry said. "You got lucky."

"Tell them," Rachel told Matt. "Tell them about the pilot."

"What pilot?" Landry asked.

Matt took a breath to collect his thoughts. "Well, we were running for the shelter in the school when we saw—"

"Matt!" a familiar voice shouted. "Rachel! Thank God!"

Matt turned to find his father running wildly toward him and Rachel, his face smudged with ash and his clothes filthy like he'd been digging in the rubble. Which judging from his tear-streaked cheeks was exactly what he'd been doing: searching the rubble, trying to find Matt and Rachel.

Then another figure appeared behind his dad.

Matt never thought he'd see his mom racing across a rubble-strewn street in her nightgown, her robe flapping like a cloak. He never thought he'd see that look on her face either; her relief at finding him and Rachel alive couldn't hide the terror she'd been feeling.

Matt's father took him and Rachel in his arms, squeezed them in a tight hug. Pain bloomed in Matt's leg, but he couldn't stop smiling anyway.

His mother touched his face and kissed Rachel's head, then wrapped all three of them in her arms. She kept saying how worried she'd been, and how happy she was, while his father just squeezed him and Rachel and wept.

"Mr. and Mrs. Dawson, I'm Private Landry of the United States Army." The American soldier stood beside them, with Chief at his heels. "I'm wondering if—"

"He's the one who found us!" Matt said.

"Actually . . ." Landry put a hand on Chief's head. "Chief is the one who found them. I wanted to ask if we could borrow him for the rest of the night. There are still people trapped."

"Borrow Chief?" Matt's father said.

"He's a natural-born search and rescue dog," Landry said. "He found your kids. Found four other people too. He saved my life."

"Goodness!" Matt's mother said. "Well, of course. Anything to help."

"He's not the only one who helped," a man with an English accent said, stepping closer.

For a moment, Matt didn't recognize him. Then he realized it was the rat-faced man—that is, the *hero*—from the cathedral roof.

"Your kids helped clear the roof," the man said.

"The cathedral roof?" Matt's father asked.

"They must have had quite a busy night," an ATS woman told the man. "Because these are the same children who led us to an injured couple."

Matt's mom squeezed him and Rachel even harder. "Looks like Chief isn't the only hero in the family."

Rachel tugged at her braid, and Matt flushed. Landry crouched to tie his makeshift leash to Chief's collar.

Firemen shouted. An ambulance picked its way down the street. Matt's exhausted gaze dragged over a man in a smock wandering from the smashed dentist's office as a horse and cart helped clear the wreckage and—

Shuffle-drag. Shuffle-drag.

Matt's blood chilled. That noise. It was the limping German pilot.

"Matt!" Rachel whispered.

Shuffle-drag.

"Where is he?" Matt asked, scanning the smoky street.

Rachel pointed with a trembling finger toward the man in the dentist's smock. Matt barely recognized the German without his flight suit, but the limp was the same, and the waterlogged boots.

"Hey!" Matt yelled. "That man—*him*—he's a German! He's a bomber!"

CHAPTER 31

"**C**hief!" Matt bellowed. "*Fetch!*"

Chief heard more than fear in Matt's voice. He heard anger.

His hackles raised, and he stood guard between Matt and Rachel. Where was the threat? The humans yapped uselessly at each other while Matt and Rachel flailed their arms.

Chief pricked his ears and . . . *there*! Footsteps! Running away. Fleeing fast between buildings— and leaving a strange scent trail. The smell of river water and engine oil and something else. Violence and . . . and *Matt*.

The man had Matt's scent on him.

A growl of fury rumbled in Chief's throat. He flashed forward. Landry wasn't stupid; he released the leash and followed Chief.

Chief's legs blurred, his muzzle lifted in a snarl. His ears pinpointed the fleeing man, and he chased him through the smoke and the rubble.

His heart pounded with the hunt. Landry and the other men followed, blocks behind.

The prey's scent changed. The man was afraid. Good.

The man scrambled into a wide-open space with a hard floor. He spun to face Chief, and a long metal tooth grew from one of his hands. Sharper than any dog's tooth.

The man crouched, raising the metal tooth—

A distant part of Chief's mind told him to wait for his pack. Wait for the men. Circle the prey-man and wait.

But a bigger part still smelled Matt's anger.

Chief didn't hesitate. He didn't break his stride. He flattened his ears and bared his teeth and ran directly at the man.

He leaped for his throat.

The metal tooth bit into Chief's side.

He felt the burn of a wound, but he didn't yelp or cringe. Instead, he slammed the man backward.

The man fell with a grunt, cracking his head on the ground.

Chief rolled and stood and bit the man's arm, the one holding the metal tooth. He shook his head like breaking a prey animal's neck, and the tooth flew. It clattered against the ground in the shadows.

Chief's side still burned, but he didn't care. He bunched his legs for another leap.

"Please!" The man dragged himself away from Chief. "Call him off, call him off!"

"Chief!" Landry ran into the open space. "Down. Down, Chief!"

Chief stalked the man, ignoring Landry's yipping.

"Call your dog off!" the prey-man wept. "Please, *bitte*! *Bitte nicht!*"

Chief didn't understand the yipping, but he approved of the sudden hardness in Landry's

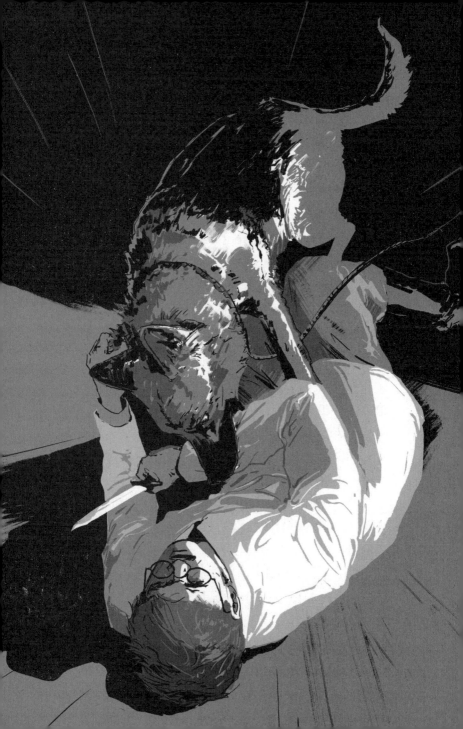

posture. The sudden wolfishness. The prey-man was an enemy.

"It is true!" the man yipped. "I surrender! The boy is right! I am a Luftwaffe bombardier."

"Well, Mr. Bombardier," Landry said, his voice smooth with threat. "If I were you, I'd keep very still."

The prey-man went motionless—except for his frightened panting.

Chief bared his teeth and eyed the man's throat. Blood soaked the fur on Chief's side. He ignored the weakness in his left leg and watched the man. Looking for any sign of defiance.

Chief felt woozy, but he stayed watchful, ready to pounce. The prey-man didn't move. Not until the rest of Landry's pack came. As Chief's leg started trembling, they dragged the prey-man to his feet and shoved him away.

"You really are a doozy," Landry told Chief. "I'd say you're the cat's meow, but I don't want to insult—"

Chief flopped to the ground, exhausted from the long night and the slash on his side.

"You're bleeding!" Landry sat beside Chief, looking at his cut. "You're hurt!"

Chief rested his head on Landry's leg, and darkness came.

CHAPTER 32

JUNE 19, 1942
2:06 P.M.

For days after the raid, smoke hung in the air above Canterbury, smelling to Matt like melted rubber and charred wood. Eight hundred buildings lay in ruins, and over five thousand more were damaged. Almost fifty people had died in the night.

But the steeple of the Canterbury Cathedral still rose above the haze.

The Nazis had wanted to destroy the cathedral. They'd wanted to break the spirit of their enemy.

They'd failed.

Hundreds of fire trucks had gathered to fight the flames during and after the raids. Civilians and soldiers banded together to help each other while firewatchers patrolling the roofs and gutters threw incendiary bombs to safety.

The cathedral still stood tall, though it bore the scars of the attack: shattered windows, a crumbling wall, and scorched lawns.

Farther down the hill, Matt crept along the hallway in his house.

Stealthy. Silent. And a little sad.

He paused outside the kitchen door and listened.

He made a face when he heard murmuring inside. He took a breath for courage, then turned the knob very slowly.

If Chief had been around, he would've noticed Matt. His ears would've pricked, and his tail would've thumped a few times. But as it was, nobody saw Matt open the door an inch and peer inside.

His mom sat with Mrs. Lloyd at the table. And the newborn baby—the noisy, red-faced infant—slept in Mrs. Lloyd's arms. Actually sleeping, for once. The baby screamed so loudly at night that Matt heard her from next door.

He called her "the Siren."

But Rachel, for some reason, found the baby adorable. She was standing next to Mrs. Lloyd right now, gazing at the little monster with misty eyes.

"Pssssst!" Matt said, staying quiet so he wouldn't risk waking the Siren.

"Yes, Matt?" his mother said in her regular voice.

"Shh! Don't wake her!" Matt looked to Rachel and whispered, "Are you coming?"

Rachel touched the baby's swaddled foot. "Is it already time?"

"Shh! Yes. *C'mon.*"

"Okay, okay." Rachel followed him into the hallway. "You are always wanting me to tag along."

"Very funny."

"Every time I turn around, there you are," she said. "A shadow."

"Shake a leg already," he told her.

She giggled and followed him outside. They

tromped through the streets—keeping away from the ruined ones—toward the park.

When they got there, they found Private Landry throwing a stick for Chief.

Chief flashed between the trees, moving smooth and strong. His coat was glossy despite the shaved patch where a vet had stitched his cut. He didn't seem to notice Matt and Rachel, except one of his ears swiveled toward them before he pounced on the stick.

Matt smiled. He liked knowing that Chief knew he was there, that Chief always kept track of him.

"Rachel, Matt!" Private Landry called. "I can't believe how fast Chief has recovered. You've taken really good care of him."

"That's nothing." Matt looked to Rachel. "Are you ready?"

She nodded and told Private Landry, "Count to a hundred. Then tell Chief to 'find.'"

Private Landry gaped at Rachel and Matt. "You've been training him?"

"One!" Matt said, jogging toward the other end of the park. "Two!"

Rachel ran beside him. "Three!"

They scrambled around a vegetable garden and through a thicket, then veered onto a path. *Thirty-five, thirty-six.*

The path curved toward the river, which smelled of geese and pond. *Fifty-seven, fifty-eight.*

Matt stopped beneath a tree and interwove his fingers. Rachel put one foot in his hands, and he boosted her onto a thick branch.

"Eighty-five," she whispered, as Matt clambered beside her. "Eighty-six . . ."

They counted the rest silently. Hiding in the tree. Quiet and still.

In the distance, Landry shouted, "Chief! Find!"

Matt held his breath. He and Rachel had trained Chief every day since the vet said he could run. And every day, Chief found the person hiding almost immediately. Then he'd look at them like they were stupid for getting lost again.

Except they'd never tried this with anyone *else* saying "find." What if Chief didn't understand? What if—

Paws rustled through fallen leaves, and a sharp bark sounded.

Chief's bright eyes watched them. Matt imagined him thinking, "How did you get lost up in a *tree*? Silly humans."

Chief barked again.

"I'm coming, I'm coming!" Landry called from farther in the park.

"Matt?" Rachel put her hand on Matt's arm. "Are you sure about this?"

"Yeah." He swallowed a lump in his throat. "It's what Eric would want."

"Yes, but what do *you* want?"

Matt felt tears in his eyes. "I understand now. I know why my parents let Eric enlist. There are things you can't ignore. Battles you can't run from. Sometimes you have to fight. Sometimes you have to give everything you've got. And Chief?"

Chief barked.

"He's not a pet, he's a soldier." Matt looked down. "A soldier dog."

When Landry jogged into sight, Matt dropped from the tree. Then he fell to his knees. He felt tears on his cheeks as he spread his arms to Chief.

Chief knew how he felt. Chief always knew. He stepped into Matt's hug and rubbed his head against Matt's chin. His fur was warm and soft.

Matt heard Rachel and Landry talking to each other, but he just held Chief and cried. After what felt like a long time, he kissed Chief's head and stood. Wiping the tears from his eyes, he reached into his shirt and pulled out the clump of cloth he'd stuffed there.

"This is for Chief," he said, giving it to Landry. "It's my pillowcase. So wherever he goes, it'll always smell like home."

Matt knew he'd cry when Chief left to join Dogs for Defense, but he also knew it was the right thing to do. For him, for Chief. And for Eric.

He felt bad about saying goodbye, and at the same time he felt good about his decision. He kept sniffling, though. And he didn't even mind when Rachel took his hand. He didn't have Chief anymore, but he wasn't alone.

Matt and Rachel walked home in silence.

Until, three doors down from their house, they heard a shriek.

"There goes the Siren again," Matt grumped.

Except it wasn't the baby crying with hunger or a wet diaper.

It was his mother, screaming with joy.

She burst from the front door waving a telegram and shouted, "They found him! They found Eric! He's okay, he's alive!"

Relief and joy exploded in Matt's heart, brighter than any bomb.

He whooped and hugged Rachel. When he spun her in circles, her braid flapped wildly, and her laughter rang out. The Canterbury air didn't stink of melted rubber and charred wood to Matt. Not anymore.

Now it smelled of hope.

DID DOGS LIKE CHIEF REALLY SERVE DURING WORLD WAR II?

Yup! When the war broke out, many Americans wanted to help—including the furry ones. Families across the country donated their dogs to a group called Dogs for Defense, who trained the brave pups to do important military tasks.

In boot camp, canine trainees learned to search for folks lost in fires and under rubble, carry cables and supplies, and alert their handlers to enemy sneak attacks. They were taught to respond to spoken commands like "FIND!" and "ATTACK!"

The character of Chief was inspired by two of WWII's bravest soldier dogs, Chips and Jet!

CHIPS

US ARMY HERO DOG

NATIONALITY: AMERICAN

BREED: GERMAN SHEPHERD-COLLIE-SIBERIAN HUSKY MIX

JOB: SENTRY DOG

STRENGTHS: BRAVERY, SPEED, LOYALTY

TRAINING: WAR DOG TRAINING CENTER IN VIRGINIA

STATIONED: EUROPE AND NORTH AFRICA

HEROIC MOMENT: RUNNING INTO MACHINE GUN FIRE AND JUMPING INTO AN ENEMY BUNKER IN ITALY TO PROTECT HIS SQUAD

HONORS: PDSA DICKIN MEDAL, BRITAIN'S HIGHEST HONOR FOR DOGS.

JET

CIVIL DEFENSE HERO DOG

NATIONALITY: BRITISH

BREED: GERMAN SHEPHERD

JOB: SEARCH AND RESCUE

STRENGTHS: BRAVERY, INTELLIGENCE, GRIT

TRAINING: GLOUCESTER WAR DOGS SCHOOL

STATIONED: LONDON

HEROIC MOMENT: SAVED MORE THAN 150 PEOPLE FROM BOMBED BUILDINGS DURING THE LONDON BLITZ

HONORS: RSPCA MEDALLION OF VALOUR AND THE PDSA DICKIN MEDAL

TOP TEN SOLDIER DOG STATS:

1. 40,000 American dogs were volunteered for the war effort.

2. The US Army used 10,000 of these patriotic pets over the course of the war.

3. The main jobs for World War II soldier dogs were sentry dogs, patrol dogs, messengers, search-and-rescue dogs, and mine-detection dogs.

4. Seven breeds were eventually accepted as the best soldier dogs: German shepherd, Belgian sheepdog, Doberman pinscher, collie, Siberian husky, malamute, and Eskimo dog.

5. Boot camp for dog soldiers lasted just as long as it did for human soldiers—eight to twelve weeks.

6. A dog's sense of smell is forty times more sensitive than a human's—making them great for search and rescue missions and sniffing out landmines and bombs!

7. A German shepherd can bite down with 238 pounds per square inch of force—that's twice as powerful as a human bite, and with sharper teeth!

8. Dogs can run at speeds of up to 30 mph.

9. The army trained dogs for use in all branches of the military.

10. Soldier dogs in training could only spend time with and be fed by their handlers, so they'd learn to tell the difference between friends and enemies.

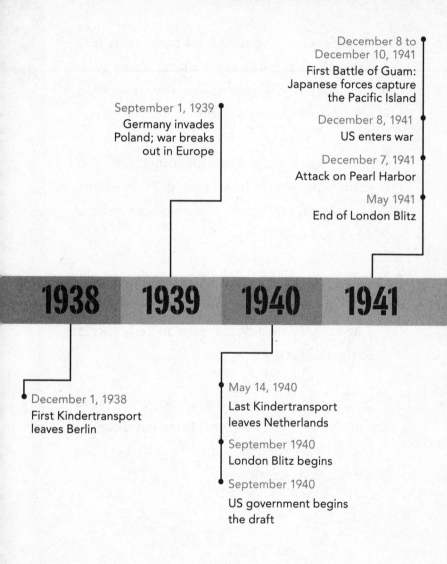

December 8 to
December 10, 1941
**First Battle of Guam:
Japanese forces capture
the Pacific Island**

December 8, 1941
US enters war

December 7, 1941
Attack on Pearl Harbor

May 1941
End of London Blitz

September 1, 1939
**Germany invades
Poland; war breaks
out in Europe**

1938 1939 1940 1941

December 1, 1938
**First Kindertransport
leaves Berlin**

May 14, 1940
Last Kindertransport
leaves Netherlands

September 1940
London Blitz begins

September 1940
US government begins
the draft

WORLD WAR II

September 2, 1945
V-J Day (Victory in Japan),
Japanese sign surrender agreement

August 14, 1945
Japanese forces surrender

August 9, 1945
Atomic bomb dropped on Nagasaki

August 6, 1945
Atomic bomb dropped on Hiroshima

May 8, 1945
V-E Day (Victory in Europe)

May 7, 1945
German forces surrender

September 1943
Italian forces surrender

1942   1943   1944   1945

January 1942
First American troops
arrive in Britain; Dogs
for Defense program is
founded

April 1942 to June 1942
Baedeker Blitz

June 1, 1942
Canterbury Blitz

July 1942
US government commits
to use of trained war dogs

August 1942
US begins work on atomic
bomb

June 6, 1944
D-Day at Normandy in
France

July 21, 1944 to
August 8, 1944
Second Battle of Guam: US
takes control from Japan

August 25, 1944
Paris is freed from German
control

Q&A ABOUT AIR RAIDS

Q. What's a blitz? Isn't that a football thing?

A. Yes, but it meant something else in World War II. "Blitz" is short for "blitzkrieg," the German word for "lightning war." During the London Blitz in 1941, German forces dropped bombs on Britain's capital every single day for three months and destroyed a third of the city. Tens of thousands of people died in these attacks, and the Luftwaffe (the German air force) dropped over 41,000 tons of bombs—that's almost a hundred MILLION pounds of bombs! (41K × 2K = 82 million)

Q. What kinds of planes did the German forces use in their attacks?

A. The Luftwaffe used several different kinds of planes for their blitzkrieg bombing—including the Heinkel, Messerschmitt, and Junkers (pronounced "yoonkers"). Each plane was used for a different kind of attack, including long-distance, nighttime, or heavy artillery.

Q. What's the difference between firebombs and incendiary bombs?

A. During the Canterbury Blitz, German bombardiers dropped two different kinds of bombs. Five-hundred-pound high-explosive firebombs burst into flames right away and were intended to blow up buildings. Incendiary bombs were used to start fires. Sometimes the chemicals inside them took a few seconds to mix together and ignite after dropping—giving the firewatchers time to throw them off the roof of the cathedral!

Q. So fire was a big threat during an air raid?

A. Yes! Volunteer firewatchers and firefighters played a huge role in protecting cities during an air raid—but sometimes the fires grew out of control! In the Canterbury Blitz, a street called Butchery Lane was used as a firebreak—a strip of open space that prevents a fire from spreading. Lucky for Canterbury, it worked! While one side of the street was destroyed in the Blitz, the other survived relatively unharmed.

Q. How did people fight back?

A. The Royal Air Force fought back in planes like the Spitfire and Beaufighter. The Spitfire was the most common British fighter plane. It seated only one pilot and was light and easy to steer through dogfights. Beaufighters were bigger, which meant they could carry more weapons and were often used in nighttime battles during the air raids. The British also used antiaircraft missiles to shoot down German planes from the ground.

Q&A ABOUT THE CANTERBURY BLITZ

Q. What was so special about the Canterbury Blitz?

A. The Canterbury Blitz was one part of a series of German attacks called the Baedeker Blitz. Germany didn't just want to win the war, it wanted to break the British spirit by destroying important historical sites in England. So the German military picked up a copy of the popular Baedeker travel guide and chose the most popular landmarks to attack. Canterbury became a target because the cathedral was built in the 1070s and many British people loved to vacation in this small coastal city.

TOP CANTERBURY BLITZ STATS:

1. Bombs began dropping on June 1, 1942, around midnight.

2. German planes dropped 130 high-explosive bombs.

3. Most of the bombs missed the historic eight-hundred-year-old cathedral because a breeze blew the flares off-target.

4. Eight hundred other buildings in Canterbury were destroyed and more than six thousand damaged.

5. More than a hundred people were injured, and forty-three died.

6. Most of the kids in Canterbury had already been evacuated through Operation Pied Piper, which began on September 1, 1939.

7. Air raids like the Canterbury Blitz came in waves—first one squadron of bombers, then a pause, then another squadron.

8. Most air-raid shelters were in the basements of homes, office buildings, and factories—and even deep within subway stations! But the main shelter in Canterbury was in the crypt beneath the cathedral.

9. Canterbury was attacked AGAIN throughout the war—135 separate raids total!

10. A total of 10,445 bombs were dropped during all the raids.

11. In the raids, 731 homes and 296 other buildings in the city were destroyed, and 115 people were killed.

12. The Canterbury Cathedral still stands.

MORE QUESTIONS ABOUT WORLD WAR II

Q. How did ATS help the war effort?

A. Keeping England safe was a team effort. Aside from groups like the air-raid wardens and firewatchers, ATS—short for Auxiliary Territorial Services—played a big role. The ATS was the women's branch of the British Army, and although they weren't allowed to serve in combat, they filled lots of important roles from communication to first aid, intelligence, military police, and radar operators. By the time the war was over, 190,000 British women had served.

Q. What was the Kindertransport?

A. "Kinder" means children in German. In this book, Rachel comes to live with Matt's family as part of the Kindertransport, a British program that saved around ten thousand Jewish kids from the Nazis. After it became clear to Great Britain that the Nazis had terrible plans for the Jewish people living in Germany and the surrounding countries, the British government found foster families for

Jewish children under the age of seventeen. The sad truth was that many of these children never saw their families again.

Q. Did the US Army and British troops really use Morse code in World War II?
A. They sure did! Morse code is the system that represents the letters of the alphabet with dots and dashes; it was invented by Samuel Morse in 1844. You had to know it to be a pilot, and it was also used for navigating at sea. Morse code was especially important to both sides in World War II because it allowed secret encrypted messages to be sent almost instantly between planes, ships, and land. In this book, Matt and Rachel use the Morse code SOS to call for help.

Join the Fight!

DON'T MISS THE NEXT
ACTION-PACKED MISSION

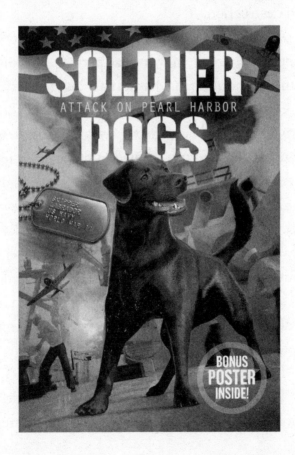

The attack came out of nowhere.

No warning, no declaration of war, no siren, before the enemy descended on the US naval base at Pearl Harbor in a wave of fire, panic, and destruction.

All across the island of Oahu, unsuspecting Americans were enjoying a perfect Hawaiian Saturday morning in what was as close to paradise on earth as one could get. Warm sunlight shone between the leaves of gently swaying palm trees. Stores and restaurants opened in preparation for a day of weekend shoppers. Hula music played softly on radios in windows and cars as coffee brewed and breakfast sizzled in pans. On the decks of the vessels of Battleship Row, a group of eight military battleships in port at the harbor, sailors were finishing up breakfasts, playing a little early catch on deck, or getting ready for a weekend's shore leave with their wives and families.

Then, the roar of plane engines.

The crackle of machine gun fire. The thunder of bombs exploding. The thud of torpedoes slamming into ship hulls beneath the rocking waves.

America was being attacked.

That was all anyone knew.

On the deck of the USS *West Virginia*, Joseph Dean, eleven years old, son of the ship's head cook, had no idea the planes raining gunfire and destruction on him and his friends were from the Empire of Japan. He didn't know that the aircraft carriers from which those planes had taken off had left Japan ten days earlier with plans to destroy Pearl Harbor. He didn't know the small black packages dropping off them were armor-piercing bombs. And he had no way of knowing that the nearby USS *Arizona* had just taken on a full 1.5 million gallons of fuel in preparation for a trip to the mainland.

All Joe knew was that Skipper, his new dog, had sensed something. She'd started barking at the edge of the ship, losing her cool in a way he'd never seen before. It had spooked them all—a warning of something they didn't understand.

A warning that came too late.

Joe saw as the planes appeared overhead. They swooped aggressively low over the ships along the Row, bathing them in bullets and bombs. Suddenly, Joe was dodging bullets and smelling smoke, and then—

BOOM!

A wall of white-hot air slammed into Joe. He flew through the air and landed on his back.

Joe sat up, dazed and hurt. Stunned, he could only watch as the *Arizona* was cut in half by a massive explosion. The ship's belly was like an opening into the pit from one of his grandmother's Bible stories, a raging fire that filled the sky with oily black smoke. As Joe tried to regain his bearings, the twenty-nine-ton battleship began to sink to the bottom of the harbor over only ten minutes, the deafening blast taking with it over a thousand American lives.

As Joe stared on in horror, Skipper appeared in front of him. She barked and barked, trying to rouse him to action. Terrified and confused, Joe threw his arms around her neck and hugged her for dear life.

"Oh, Skipper," he cried, his body shaking against hers, "what's going on? Who's attacking us, girl? How did this happen?"